She wanted to hurt him

"You know your trouble, Mr. Big Shot Adams?" she said, sneering in reply. "You can't stand the thought that I might have preferred Fergus to you."

"Well, neither of us got what we wanted in the end, did we?" he responded. "Tell me, what happened to sailor boy? Couldn't he take it when you had *my* bastard, not his?"

"Don't call Rory a bastard!" Riona cried back.

"Why? It's you who made him one," he accused with hard contempt.

Riona flinched visibly, accepting the truth of what he'd said. If she had taken his advice, there would have been no baby.

They stared at each other for a moment, the worst kind of enemies—the kind who had once been lovers—then he crossed to the door and departed without a word.

ALISON FRASER was born in Scotland, but now lives in England with her husband, two children and two dogs. After specializing in English and Social Sciences at Aberdeen University, she taught mathematics for five years, then was a computer programmer for an engineering firm. Her first book, written as relaxation from work, was not publishable, but she persisted. Though she says writing doesn't come easily, she enjoys the idea of people gaining pleasure from her books. Reading, bridge and backgammon are among her other interests.

Books by Alison Fraser

HARLEQUIN PRESENTS
697—PRINCESS
721—THE PRICE OF FREEDOM
745—COMING HOME
865—A MAN WORTH KNOWING
1135—A LIFETIME AND BEYOND
1425—TIME TO LET GO

Don't miss any of our special offers. Write to us at the following address for information on our newest releases.

Harlequin Reader Service
U.S.: 3010 Walden Ave., P.O. Box 1325, Buffalo, NY 14269
Canadian: P.O. Box 609, Fort Erie, Ont. L2A 5X3

ALISON FRASER

Love Without Reason

Harlequin Books

TORONTO • NEW YORK • LONDON
AMSTERDAM • PARIS • SYDNEY • HAMBURG
STOCKHOLM • ATHENS • TOKYO • MILAN
MADRID • WARSAW • BUDAPEST • AUCKLAND

ISBN 0-373-11675-6

LOVE WITHOUT REASON

Copyright © 1993 by Alison Fraser.

This edition published by arrangement with Harlequin Enterprises B. V.

Printed in U.S.A.

CHAPTER ONE

'Is IT mine?' were his very first words, when they met outside the village store.

Riona stood a moment, caught by memories. It had been over a year and she'd never expected to see him again. She wasn't ready for this.

She murmured a faint 'What?' in response.

'The baby you've had—is it mine?' he repeated coolly.

No 'It's good to see you!' No 'How are you?' Just straight to the point for Cameron Adams.

'No, it isn't.' She gave him the answer he wanted.

It was a surprise that he even bothered adding, 'Are you sure?'

She nodded.

They stood a moment longer, looking at each other, remembering...

Then Riona turned to walk away.

He blocked her path.

'In that case——' his lips formed a contemptuous curve '—I guess Fergus Ross is the lucky man.'

'You can guess what you like,' Riona threw back, and pushed past him.

He let her go and she hurried up the road, turning a couple of times to check he wasn't following. He remained outside the shop, watching her retreat. He probably thought she was running away from him—and he was right.

She was out of breath when she reached Dr Macnab's house. She rang the bell with some urgency.

'He's back, Doctor,' she gasped as the door opened. 'I just met him. At the store. He's heard about Rory. I have to go——'

'Now, calm down, lass,' Dr Macnab advised, leading her inside. 'You mean Cameron Adams?'

She nodded, before going to pick up the baby lying on the living-room carpet. He gave her a beautiful toothless smile.

'Cameron knows about the lad here.' Dr Macnab was clearly less distressed by the fact. 'Then he must have come to help you. I was certain he would. If only you'd let me write him——'

'No, Doctor.' Riona shook her head. 'I don't know why he's come, but it's not to help. More likely he's scared I'll bring a paternity suit against him.'

'Ah, Riona, lass.' The old doctor sighed at her cynicism. 'I can't think that's so. He took advantage of you, it's true, but he's not a bad man. Now he knows he's fathered Rory——'

'Actually, he doesn't,' Riona stated, before the doctor's optimism could carry him away.

'But you said...' Hamish Macnab tried to remember exactly what she had said.

'Someone told him I'd had a baby,' Riona explained. 'He wanted to know if it was his. I said it wasn't.'

'*What?*' The old man was plainly shocked.

'I just told him what he wanted to hear, Doctor,' Riona justified her actions. 'You won't tell him differently, will you?'

'I can't. You know that.' As her doctor, he couldn't break a confidence, even if he wished to. 'But, lass, you can't hope to get away with it. He just has to see Rory...'

Riona frowned at this mention of the likeness between baby and father. She adored her son, but that was how she thought of him—*her* son, and nobody else's.

'I'll make sure he doesn't.' Her jaw set with determination as she dressed the baby in his outdoor clothes and went to put him in the carrier she used.

Dr Macnab stopped her, saying, 'Come away, lass, I'll give you a lift.'

She accepted the offer. It was quite a walk back to her crofthouse and she didn't want to risk a second meeting with Cameron Adams.

Unfortunately the doctor used the car journey to try and persuade her to tell the truth to the American. She listened politely and, on parting, agreed to think about it, knowing full well she wouldn't. A year ago Cameron Adams had returned to Boston without a word or a backward glance. He'd left her with a breaking heart and a baby on the way. In time her heart had hardened and life now centred on her son; they needed no help from his father.

She carried young Rory into the crofthouse and sat him in a bouncing cradle close to the old-fashioned range. When they weren't out on the hills, they inhabited the kitchen, because it was the warmest room.

Rory had actually been born in the house. He'd arrived a few weeks early, allowing no time to travel to hospital in Inverness, and Dr Macnab had delivered him in the bedroom upstairs. He had been a healthy eight pounds, the birth had been relatively easy, and love for her son had flowed through her from the moment he'd been placed in her arms. Giving him up would have been impossible.

Yet keeping him sometimes seemed an act of selfishness. She looked round her shabby kitchen, furnished with an ill-assorted collection of sideboards and tables from her granny's day. Some work had recently been done by the estate to try and eradicate damp in the walls and warm up the cold stone floor with linoleum, but it was still a shabby place. It made her realise how little she had to offer Rory. She didn't even own the small, cheerless house, and she barely eked a living from working the croft. She carried Rory with her when she herded the sheep, and, despite the doctor's assurances, she worried that the fresh air was too bracing for a five-month-old baby.

It wasn't just the practical difficulties, either. For herself, she could put up with the gossip and the disapproving looks, but what would happen when the boy was older? The peninsula of Invergair might cover a wide area, but its society was narrow. An illegitimate baby was still a talking-point, especially when the father's identity was uncertain, and in time Rory would be the one to suffer. She had considered leaving the West Coast for Edinburgh, but she would have to find a place to stay and a job to do, and there wasn't much call for crofters in the city. So she stayed in Invergair, living the life of a virtual recluse.

Of course she couldn't do that forever, couldn't keep her son hidden away from curious eyes. She just hoped that, given time, the likeness to his father would fade enough to pass unnoticed.

It seemed a vain hope, however, as she cradled her son in her arms. He had a shock of black hair, dark blue eyes and the hint of a dimple in his chin. All babies were born with blue eyes, she'd been told, but his would stay blue. She knew this because her son was a tiny replica of his father.

Cameron Adams. The thought of their meeting today sent a chill through her. His directness had always been disconcerting. Now it seemed brutal. She supposed he'd been angry about the baby; he'd done his best to ensure there would be no consequences from their brief affair. Even as he'd talked of a future together, he'd known all along it would never be.

Riona's mind slipped back once more to last summer. It had mainly been a good summer, warm and dry and sunny, but not on the June day they'd met. Then it had been raining. She'd been returning from her weekly trip to Inverness and had caught the bus that went as far as Achnagair. She had started walking home the six more miles to Invergair, hoping for a lift from a local, when a car slid to a halt beside her. It was a posh car, a sleek black BMW. An electric window rolled down and the driver leaned over the passenger-seat to speak to her. She stood a cautious step or two from the door.

'Hey, kid, am I on the right road for Invergair?' the driver called to her.

She nodded in response, but didn't volunteer more.

'How far is it, do you reckon?' he pursued.

She answered, 'Six miles to the village,' but was careful to keep her voice low. Dressed in jeans and hooded jacket, she'd been taken for a boy. It seemed wise to maintain the illusion.

'So, it's straight on?' he concluded.

She nodded again, and, stepping back from the car, resumed walking.

Instead of driving on, however, he drew up in a lay-by slightly ahead of her, and, climbing out of the car, called back, 'You might as well hitch a ride, kid.'

'I . . .' Riona hesitated, torn between saving herself the walk and the potential risk. She looked him up and down, struck first by his size. He was well over six feet and looked muscular in build, despite expensively cut clothes. Riona knew little or nothing about designer labels, but she could still recognise money even when it walked around in casual suede jackets and faded jeans.

He also happened to be the most attractive man Riona had ever met. Her eyes went from his clothes to his face and just stayed there. With thick dark hair above straight dark brows, a long nose and square, unshaven jaw, he looked both handsome and dangerous. Then, all of a sudden, his hard, beautiful mouth slanted into a half-smile and his dark blue eyes glittered with cynical amusement.

'Do you want references, kid?' he suggested at her lengthy scrutiny. 'A ride, that's all I'm offering. Take it or leave it.'

'OK.' Riona opened the passenger door and cautiously slid into the passenger seat, gripping her holdall to her.

'Relax, kid. Boys aren't my thing,' he said with a short laugh.

Riona felt herself blushing and was glad her jacket hood hid much of her face. She decided to keep it on.

He didn't seem to notice. He set the car in motion before asking, 'Are you from Invergair?'

'Yes,' she replied simply.

'How big is the village?'

'Not very.'

'A one-horse town,' he remarked in a drawl. 'That's what we'd call it in the States.'

'Really.' Riona sounded less than interested in what an American would call Invergair.

Her reticence was noted, as he came back with a wry, 'So tell me, are all the locals as gabby as you?'

'I . . .' Stuck for an answer, Riona glanced at him, then looked away as a mocking brow was lifted in her direction.

Of course he was right. She was being ungracious. Riona realised that. He hadn't needed to offer her a lift. He didn't even know she was a girl. It was she who was over-conscious of him as a man.

Silence descended until they approached the turn-off for Invergair, then she deepened her voice slightly to request, 'Could you let me off here? My croft's further on.'

He slowed down, saying, 'How far?'

'A mile or so.' She nodded towards the road ahead.

'Then I might as well take you.' He shrugged, and, before she could object, picked up speed once more.

'Thanks,' she murmured reluctantly. She didn't want to be the recipient of such generosity, particularly when she'd been so churlish herself. 'You can drop me here, please,' she said after they'd travelled the further mile.

He slowed down again, but, seeing no sign of habitation, asked, 'Where do you live, kid?'

'On the hill.' She pointed at the rough dirt track leading towards her croft, then found herself protesting, 'No, don't go up it!'

'Why not?' He'd already turned on to the track.

'Well...' Riona searched for a reason, other than an unwillingness to let him see her home '...the track isn't tarred. Your car might be damaged.'

'So? It's a rental.' He casually dismissed the gleamingly expensive motor car and continued up the rutted road to the crofthouse.

The rain had ceased and, as they reached the top of the hill, they had a clear view of her cottage. Built of rough stone and slate tiles, it could be described neither as cute nor quaint. It was a drab, plain building, with a kitchen and sitting-room downstairs, and two bedrooms in the attic. Round it was a dry stone wall, half falling down, and a garden that had gone to weed. The air of neglect was emphasised by the fact that it was deserted.

'Where are your folks?' the American asked as they drew to a halt and no one came out to greet them.

'I haven't any.' Riona's parents had died in an accident when she was too young to remember them. The grandfather who'd raised her had died in the past year.

'So who looks after you?' he pursued, when she made to climb out of the car.

'No one. I look after myself.' Riona wondered how old he thought her.

He stared hard at her for the first time. She stared back. It was a mistake.

Before she could stop him, he pulled down her hood and announced with some disbelief, 'Hell, you're a girl!'

Riona could hardly deny it. Under the hood, her blonde hair was bound in a long, thick plait, and, though she wore no make-up, her soft skin and the full curve of her mouth made her utterly feminine.

'Beautiful, too,' he added under his breath.

Riona ignored it. Her grandfather had taught her to consider beauty a doubtful quality.

'I'm also twenty and quite able to fend for myself, thank you,' she announced rather briskly, and reached for the door-handle.

He caught her arm, detaining her. 'You're on your own here?'

Riona frowned at the question, not sure how to answer. He was still a stranger and it didn't seem too clever to admit to being alone.

'Not really,' she eventually said. 'There's Jo. He lives with me.'

'Jo?' He repeated the name, before guessing wrongly, 'Your husband?'

Riona didn't contradict him but her blush gave her away.

'Not your husband,' he concluded drily, before shrugging. 'Never mind. Who gets married these days?'

If he was trying to save her embarrassment, he drew a scowl for his trouble. Riona didn't need his approval for living with a man, especially when she wasn't—Jo was her collie dog.

'Have I said something wrong?' he continued at her hostile silence. 'You want to get married and he doesn't. Is that it?'

'What?' Riona couldn't believe the nerve of him.

He went on obliviously, 'Well, if you want my opinion, he needs his head examined . . . his eyesight, too.'

Once more he admired her beauty, his gaze warm and approving, but any compliment was lost on Riona.

Gritting her teeth, she retorted, 'Actually, this may come as a surprise to you, Mr . . .'

'Cameron,' he supplied.

'Mr Cameron, but——' she tried to continue.

He cut in again. 'No, Cameron's my first name.'

'Mr Whatever-your-name is, then!' Riona snapped in exasperation. 'The point is I *don't* want your opinion. I'll probably never want your opinion. In fact, I can't think of anyone's opinion I'd want less!' she declared on a strident note and jerked her arm free.

'Thank you for the lift,' she added gruffly, and got out of the car before he could stop her. He climbed out, too, but remained on the driver's side, returning her slightly alarmed look with a smile. The smile suggested he hadn't taken offence. Riona thought that was a great pity.

She glowered back at him, and he drawled, 'Say, has anyone ever told you how beautiful you look when you're mad...? Because if they have, I'm afraid they were lying,' he declared in amused tones. 'That incredibly sexy mouth goes into a thin, grumpy line. And your eyes, well, they go from a green reminiscent of——'

'This is absurd!' Riona finally interrupted the running commentary. 'Look, I'm grateful for the lift, but it doesn't give you discussion rights on my private life or my appearance. So if you don't mind...?'

She looked from him to the track down the hill, and waited for him to take the hint.

He did eventually, concluding, 'I guess that means I'm not being invited in for coffee.'

'Astute as well as sensitive,' Riona muttered under her breath.

He caught it and laughed. 'Well, never mind, I'll take a raincheck.'

Then, while Riona was still working on a reply, he gave a half-salute with his hand and climbed back into the car. She watched as he drove down the track, faster than he should, and found herself almost wishing an accident on him. Not a big accident. Just one where he and his flash car ended up in the ditch.

It was hardly a nice thing to imagine, but Riona didn't feel very nice at that moment. Grumpy, indeed! And what about the conclusions he'd leapt to? Not only did he have her living with some man, but he'd also decided she was desperate for marriage.

That his conclusions were ridiculous didn't matter. It was his sheer presumption that maddened her. She thought of all the clever things she might have said and hadn't, and for a moment hoped they *would* meet again. Then she shook her head at the possibility. In a couple of days the American would have 'done' Invergair and be on his way, further north to Gairloch, or back down south to some posh hotel. No tourist ever stayed long in their area.

She'd been wrong, of course. Cameron Adams hadn't just passed through. He had been there a month in all— just long enough to change her life for ever.

The next time she'd seen him was that night at the ceilidh in the village hall. It was a weekly event in the summer, a mixture of song, dancing and recitation that brought crofters from all over the peninsula of Invergair.

Riona had to attend the ceilidh because, when her grandfather had fallen ill, she'd taken his place playing piano in the band, the other members being two local fishermen on fiddle and accordion. Their repertoire consisted solely of dancing reels, but she'd never been a musical snob. She was needed to play, and play she did.

She'd just finished a Dashing White Sergeant and had come off stage for a break, when she spotted the American. She could hardly fail to, as he bore down on her, allowing no chance of escape.

'I've just spent the last half-hour looking for you,' he said without preamble.

Riona matched his directness with a flat 'Really. Why?'

He laughed in response. She wondered if he ever took offence—and, if so, how she could possibly give it.

He went on obliviously, 'I didn't notice the piano player. As a rule, they don't tend to be so beautiful.'

Riona ignored the compliment, but couldn't ignore his eyes. They slid from her face to the dress she wore. A simple bodiced dress in white cotton, it left her arms and shoulders bare and kept her cool in the warm, crowded hall. It also hinted at the first swell of her breasts, a fact that she hadn't really noticed until the American's gaze lingered there.

Riona had always found her figure an embarrassment. She didn't mind being tall—at five nine, she was taller than many Highland males. And, in her usual clothes of baggy jerseys and jeans, it hardly mattered what her figure was like. She just wished that, when she wore feminine clothes, her curves were less pronounced, less suggestive. It seemed a joke of nature when, in character, she wasn't the 'sexy type' at all.

She felt only anger as the American's eyes reflected his thoughts, and she snapped, 'Perhaps I can have my dress back when you've finished.'

'What?' Distracted from their private fantasy, his eyes travelled back to her face, and he gave her one of his slow smiles. 'I guess I was being obvious.'

'Painfully,' she agreed, and tried to walk past him.

He moved to block her path. 'So can I buy you a drink?'

'No, thank you,' she said, politeness forced. 'I don't drink.'

'You're kidding.' His face expressed genuine surprise. 'Next to bagpipe playing and caber-tossing, I thought drinking was the national pastime in Scotland.'

Not sure if this was meant to be a joke or what, Riona scowled in response.

She countered, 'So why did you come if you have such a low opinion of the place?'

'On the contrary——' he shook his head '—I think it's a wonderful country. Drunk or sober, no one can rival the Scots for their generosity of spirit. It makes you quite forget their occasional bloody-mindedness,' he said on a wry note.

Again he was probably joking, but Riona wasn't laughing. 'Do you know what I like about you Americans?' she rallied.

'No, what?' He actually smiled.

'Your stunning diplomacy,' she answered with dead-pan sarcasm, then smiled, too—before walking away.

She was intercepted again, but this time by Dr Macnab. 'Well, good evening, lass,' he greeted her, then added, 'I see you've met him.'

'Who?'

'The American.'

'Oh, him.' Riona pulled a face.

'You didn't like him?' The doctor frowned.

'Not so you'd notice,' she shrugged back. 'I just hope the new laird isn't like him.'

The Doctor's frown changed to a look of puzzlement, before he sighed, 'I'm rather afraid he is, lass.'

It took Riona a moment to catch on. They'd been waiting months for the new laird's arrival, ever since Sir Hector had finally pegged out at ninety-five. They'd heard he was an American, a C H Adams from Boston, and that was about it. They'd worked out for themselves that he wasn't too interested in his inheritance, having failed to materialise to claim it in person.

'You don't mean...' Riona prayed she'd misunderstood.

She hadn't, as the doctor went on, 'Aye, that's the man himself. Sir Hector's great-nephew.'

'Oh, God!' Riona closed her eyes in despair. She had just cut dead the man who owned the cottage in which she lived and the croft she worked.

'What's wrong?' the doctor asked.

'Nothing really.' Riona grimaced. 'I was just rather insulting to him.'

'Dearie me,' Dr Macnab exclaimed in his mild way. 'That's not like you. He must have said something to prompt it.'

Riona nodded, before pointing out, 'But that hardly matters. He's laird and I'm just a lowly tenant... least, I *was*.'

'Ach, lass,' the doctor chided, 'he's no going to turf you out for a few hasty words. In fact, he's probably laughed them off already. I'm told he's got a fine sense of humour.'

Riona gave an unladylike snort. Fine wasn't the word she'd have used—more like warped.

'Who told you that?' she asked.

'Mrs Ross.' The doctor named his housekeeper. 'Her sister's girl, Morag, helps with the cleaning up at the House.'

The House was Invergair Hall, the seat of the Munro family. It wasn't quite a castle, but it did boast a turret or two and was fairly imposing in size.

'Anyway, Morag thinks he's very charming,' Dr Macnab continued.

'Yes, well...' Riona wasn't too impressed with Morag Mackinnon's opinion. A nice enough girl, her head was easily turned by a good-looking male, and Riona supposed Cameron Adams was that.

She glanced round the hall and located him without difficulty. Over six feet, he was the tallest man there. His dark handsome head was inclined in conversation with Isobel Fraser, the secretary to the estate and Invergair's resident vamp. At thirty-three, she'd already seen off two husbands in the divorce courts.

'Isobel seems to like him, too,' Dr Macnab chuckled. 'Perhaps she's measuring him up for number three.'

'She's welcome,' Riona replied tartly.

'Ach, you wouldna wish Isobel on him,' the doctor said, still with gentle humour. 'A bonny lass she may be, but she has a hard heart.'

Riona didn't disagree, muttering instead, 'I wouldn't worry too much about Cameron Adams, Doctor. He didn't strike me as the vulnerable type.'

'Perhaps not,' the doctor conceded, before relaying, 'At any rate, he told old Mrs Mackenzie, the house-keeper at the Hall, he wasn't the marrying kind.'

'Really?' The news didn't surprise Riona. She remembered his showing a healthy contempt for the married state the first time they'd met.

Dr Macnab went on to explain, 'Apparently a Mrs Adams called from America while he was out and Mrs Mackenzie assumed it was his wife. He laughed at the idea, saying that Mrs Adams was his stepmother, and that acquiring a wife was something he'd so far managed to avoid.'

The doctor smiled, amused by the American's phrasing, while Riona declared cynically, 'I suspect they've avoided him—women with any taste, that is.'

'Oh, I don't know.' The doctor gazed across to where the American was standing, having attracted another couple of ladies into his circle. 'He seems to be charming the birds out of the trees.'

Riona glanced at the American again and made a dismissive sound. True, he appeared to be gaining a fan club, but they were women who would have fluttered round the new laird if he'd turned out to be the devil himself.

'I hope he doesn't expect us all to fawn on him,' she muttered aloud, refusing to be susceptible to those powerful good looks.

'I'm sure he doesn't,' Dr Macnab said more reasonably. 'At least, I can't think he'll be any worse than Sir Hector.'

'Mmm.' A non-committal sound from Riona. True, Sir Hector had been a terrible old autocrat with a variable temper and an almost feudal attitude to his tenants, but who knew what his successor was really like?

Feeling she'd already wasted too much time discussing the American, Riona excused herself and returned to the stage with the rest of the band. They continued through their repertoire of dance numbers. It was music Riona could have played in her sleep, which was fortunate as her attention kept wandering back to Cameron Adams.

She saw him dancing the Highland schottische with Isobel Fraser. They were both dreadful at it. Isobel was actually a lowlander from Strathclyde and normally considered herself too sophisticated for the weekly ceilidh. It wasn't hard to guess what had brought her to this one.

When the other two band members suggested playing a slow, romantic air, Riona shook her head and led the music into an eightsome reel. Then, in an unusually spiteful mood, she enjoyed watching Isobel try to keep up with the energetic dance. High heels and reels did not go together. The couple eventually left the floor, mid-dance, and, losing sight of them, Riona assumed they had gone completely.

Only later, when the dance was over and she went in search of a lift from the doctor, did she discover the two men—Dr Macnab and Cameron Adams—making each other's acquaintance at a table in the far corner of the hall. She stopped in her tracks and was about to retreat altogether when the older man spotted her.

'Ah, Riona,' Dr Macnab hailed her, and she reluctantly approached the table. 'I was just about to come and look for you. You'll be wanting a lift?'

'Aye, Doctor, if it's not too much trouble,' she said stiltedly, inhibited by the American's presence.

She didn't have to look to know his eyes were boring into her. But she looked all the same and immediately regretted it.

'I'll give you a lift,' the American said in a tone that suggested refusal wasn't an option.

Riona's heart sank. She'd sooner walk the four miles in bare feet.

It was Dr Macnab who answered warmly, 'That's good of you, Cameron,' when Riona remained silent.

'It's on my way.' Cameron Adams dismissed any kindness in the offer, then directed at Riona, 'Are you ready?'

What could she say? Remembering her first lift with him, she'd no wish to repeat the experience. But he *was* the new laird, while *she* was just one of his tenants.

'It is good of you,' she echoed the doctor, 'but it's not really your most direct route. If you go west from the village, it's about five miles to the House. You have to go in a circle to pass my croft and it almost doubles the journey.'

'Yeah, I know,' was his only response, as he placed a hand at her elbow, and, with a last, 'See you around, Doc,' to the older man, began steering her towards the door.

The hall was still busy with people saying goodbye and Riona felt every one of them was staring in their direction. By tomorrow it would be round the village— Riona Macleod had left the ceilidh with the new laird. She could imagine what the gossips might conclude from that.

Cameron Adams smiled disarmingly at people they passed and raised a hand in farewell to Isobel Fraser, who was trapped in conversation with the local vet. He swept on towards the door, without noticing Isobel frantically signalling in return.

'I think Isobel's trying to catch your attention,' Riona told him. 'Maybe she needs a lift. I could go with the doctor...'

'Uh-huh, forget it,' he dismissed, marching her towards his BMW. 'Isobel has her own transport, and, even if she didn't, I don't think she'd be short of a man to take her home... So be a good girl, stop arguing, and just get in,' he added, as they reached his car and he opened the passenger door for her.

Riona felt mutinous at his 'good girl' and wondered what he'd do if she took to her heels instead. She looked around for a bolt-hole.

'I wouldn't if I were you.' He read her perfectly. 'Unless, of course, you'd like to be dragged back, caveman style.'

'You'd not dare!' she retorted angrily.

He smiled. 'Try me.'

Riona was tempted, almost certain he must be bluffing. It would be more embarrassing for him—the new laird seen accosting a local girl outside the village hall. That was assuming, of course, that Cameron Adams ever got embarrassed.

He continued to smile down at her until Riona decided he would dare, and got into the car.

He quickly climbed into the other side and switched on the engine. Then, before driving off, he turned to say, 'Your safety-belt—put it on.'

It was definitely an order, not a suggestion.

Riona muttered rebelliously, 'Why? Am I going to need it?' remembering how fast he drove.

He ignored the comment and repeated, 'Put it on!'

Riona, who had simply forgotten the belt, took exception, not to it, but to his tone. She decided she would do up the belt in her own sweet time.

But it seemed Cameron Adams wasn't prepared to wait that long, as he leaned over her to grasp the strap and, drawing it across her front, locked it into position. In doing so, the back of his hand brushed against her breast. While Riona felt almost panicked by the contact, he didn't seem to notice, and calmly turned back to grip the wheel and set the car in motion.

Riona seethed in silence. She had never met anyone so arrogant. Who did he think he was?

She asked herself the question and answered it in the same breath. He was the laird—and what in heaven's name was she doing arguing with him? Did she want to be thrown off her croft, after trying so hard to keep it going for the past two years?

She'd lived there almost her whole life. Her parents, both music teachers, had died in a car accident when she was two, and her grandparents had taken her home to live with them. She was ten when her granny had died, and then it had just been her and her grandpa. Later she'd had the chance of a place at music college in Edinburgh, but she'd chosen to stay with him instead. He'd been in his mid-seventies by then, and growing frail. She'd nursed him through a series of debilitating strokes until a final one had brought release for him. She had not considered it release for herself. Six months on, she still missed the old man who'd brought her up and cared for her in his own tough, uncompromising way.

'So where was Jo tonight?' The American's drawl brought her back to the present.

'Jo?' She didn't understand.

'You know—the boyfriend,' he helped her out.

That Jo, Riona groaned inwardly, recalling the lie she'd told.

'Doesn't he like dancing?' the man pursued.

'Eh—no,' Riona could say with some vestige of truth. Collies didn't tend to go in for dancing.

'Two left feet, has he?' the American drawled on. 'Or should I say four?'

Four? It was a second before Riona caught on. He knew!

'Who told you?'

'Dr Macnab... After some confusion, not to mention amusement, on the doctor's side, I realised Jo was more into rounding up sheep than dancing.'

'Oh,' Riona muttered faintly.

'*Oh*?' he echoed this rather inadequate explanation.

Remembering who he was, she felt obliged to add, 'I suppose I should apologise.'

'Not if it's going to kill you,' he said at her forced admission. 'An explanation will do. Like why you let me believe you were shacked up with some guy.'

'I didn't!' Riona protested, quickly forgetting who he was. 'You asked if I lived alone. I mentioned Jo and your imagination filled in the rest.'

'You could have told me differently,' he pointed out.

'Oh, yes. That would have been very clever. Telling a complete stranger I lived in a lonely crofthouse all on my own,' she retorted angrily, then, seeing they'd come to her turn-off, snapped, 'You can let me off here.'

'I can, but I'm not going to,' was his answer, as he turned up the hill track and drove right to the door of the croft.

The moment the car stopped, Riona scrambled out with a perfunctory, 'Thanks for the lift.'

But he climbed out, too, coming round to her side of the car. 'You're right about it being lonely up here. I'll see you inside, check you have no intruders.'

'There's no need.' She wanted him gone. He made her more nervous than any potential intruder.

He sensed it, saying, 'Relax, this isn't move one in a grand seduction plan. Even assuming I like my women hard to get along with—which I don't—you're far too young for me.'

In theory Riona should have been relieved at this announcement. In practice, she was stung into replying, 'Or maybe you're just too old for me.'

But if she'd wanted to offend him, she didn't succeed. He gave a short laugh before drawling, 'Strike that "hard to get along with"; make it "damn nigh impossible".' Then he grabbed hold of her arm and steered her towards the door of her cottage.

He breathed down her neck while she unlocked the door and didn't give her a chance to shut it on him. Resigned, she led the way through the small front hall to the living-room, switching on lights as she went.

She turned to find him surveying the room with an expression of disbelief on his face. Riona understood well enough. Poverty was reflected in the threadbare furniture and carpets, the shabbiness of her home, but she refused to be ashamed of it.

She tilted her head and dared him to comment.

Instead he said simply, 'If you'd like to make us a cup of coffee, I promise not to take it as an invitation.'

'To what?' she asked rather foolishly.

He smiled at her naïveté. 'To outstay my welcome, let's say.'

Riona continued to frown. As far as she was concerned, he already had.

'I only have tea,' she said ungraciously.

'That'll do.' He shrugged in reply.

Left with no choice, Riona went through to the kitchen at the back, where her grandfather's collie greeted her with much tail-wagging before taking an alert stance as the American appeared behind her.

If he'd thought the living-room bad, Riona knew he'd find the kitchen worse. The linoleum was peeling, the table and chairs rickety, and the cooking range large, ugly and ancient.

He looked round with a critical eye, but again refrained from commenting, nodding towards the collie instead.

'Jo, I presume.' He bent to offer the collie a hand to sniff.

'Yes, but he doesn't much take to strangers,' she responded, as the collie backed away to his basket in the corner.

'Like dog, like mistress,' the American drawled in an undertone intended to be heard.

Riona refused to justify herself. No, she didn't like strangers. Not over-familiar ones, at any rate, she thought, as he leaned his considerable length against her granny's old dresser.

'Jo's my grandfather's dog, actually,' she replied coolly.

'Your grandfather,' he echoed. 'Yes, Dr Macnab said he'd died recently.'

Busy with the tea things, Riona gave a brief nod that discouraged further interest in her private life.

Or would have done, if Cameron Adams hadn't been so thick-skinned. 'It must be difficult, running this place on your own,' he continued, oblivious.

'I manage,' she countered, wondering what he was getting at. Perhaps it wasn't just casual conversation. 'I won't fall behind in my rent, Mr Adams, if that's what's worrying you.'

'*Cameron*,' he insisted, 'and no, I wasn't worrying about your rent. From what I've seen of the accounts, I doubt it's worth worrying about,' he added with a short laugh.

Riona did not laugh back. What did he mean? Did he consider the rents too low? She could barely pay the present amount.

Her face revealed her thoughts, as Cameron Adams drawled, 'Relax, kid. Whatever you pay for this place, it's probably too much.'

He cast a disparaging glance round the kitchen.

Riona was caught between reactions: relief there'd be no rent rise versus anger at the insult to her home.

Powerless to argue, she confined herself to asking how he liked his tea, before placing it unceremoniously on the dresser beside him. She didn't invite him to sit, and didn't sit herself, instead taking a stance by the sink, as far from him as possible. Being a small kitchen, it wasn't very far, and she felt overly conscious of him.

He stared back at her, without any attempt to pretend he was doing otherwise, and she dropped her eyes to the worn linoleum.

'Does the boyfriend help?' he suddenly asked.

'What?' She looked at him blankly.

He repeated, 'The boyfriend. Does he help with the croft?'

She narrowed her eyes. How much did he know of her life?

'Who says I have a boyfriend?'

'It's not a secret, is it?'

He smiled at her caginess. She frowned in response.

'He's in the Navy, isn't he?' he said, as if her memory might need jogging.

Of course she'd realised whom he meant. Fergus Ross. But who had told him? Surely not Dr Hamish?

'So how serious is it?' he asked, when she remained silent.

'I...I...' His directness was unbelievable. 'Why do you want to know?'

He shrugged, before saying, 'I guess I'm interested, after all.'

'In what?' Riona genuinely didn't understand.

'In you,' the American replied simply.

He was joking. He had to be, Riona decided, as she gave him a disgruntled look and he flashed her a brilliant smile in return. He was just trying to disconcert her.

'It's against my better judgement, of course,' he continued in the same vein. 'I mean you're really not my type. That's not to say you aren't beautiful. You are. *Very*.'

He paused to give her a look that made Riona wish she'd kept her coat on. 'Do you expect me to be flattered?'

'Hell, no,' he said, clearly amused by the conversation, 'I expect the boys have been queuing up to tell you you're beautiful for a few years now.... I suppose all the practice has helped you perfect that put-down manner of yours.'

'Why, you...' Riona searched furiously for a suitable insult to trade, then remembered once more whom she was talking to.

He lifted a dark brow, prompting. 'Yes?'

'I...you...this isn't fair!' she finally protested.

'Fair?' he echoed.

'You can stand there, saying what you want,' Riona ran on, 'and I have to stand here, taking it, because you're laird, and I'm not.'

'What?' He'd obviously not thought of it from that angle, and, when he did, he laughed out loud. 'How feudal. You think you can't argue back, because I'm your landlord. What do you imagine I'm going to do? Throw you out on the street?'

Put like that, it did sound absurd, and Riona went on the defensive. 'I don't know. Your great-uncle wasn't too keen on people disagreeing with him.'

'So I've gathered——' the American shrugged '—but I'm not Sir Hector. And, despite its attractions, I don't believe in *droit de seigneur*.'

'What?' Riona had never heard the phrase.

'*Droit de seigneur*?' he repeated, and, at her clear ignorance, went on to explain, 'In olden days, I believe the local lord in an area had the right to sleep with village maidens the night before they married. Unfortunately the custom's been out of fashion for a few centuries. However, if you fancy reviving it...' he suggested with a lascivious smile that definitely made a joke of it.

Riona felt she should be disgusted, but wasn't. In fact, for a moment she actually pictured it, two figures entwined on a big four-poster in Invergair Hall. She blushed at the direction her imagination had taken her and looked away from those sharp blue eyes of his.

'I don't suppose you're planning on marrying soon,' he added with the same undercurrent of laughter.

'No, I am not!' Riona declared on an emphatic note.

'Not serious, then,' he concluded in reply.

'About what?' She was slow to catch up.

'About Fergus Ross.' He had brought them full circle back to the question he'd originally asked.

Riona had answered it, without realising, by denying any marriage plans. The smug look of satisfaction on his face was maddening.

It prompted her to claim, 'You can be serious without wanting marriage. Maybe I don't believe in it.'

'That's OK. Neither do I.' He smiled as if they'd just come to some agreement, and straightened his length from the dresser.

He took a step in her direction and Riona found herself backed against the sink. She garbled out, 'As a matter of fact, Fergus and I do have an understanding.'

'Really.' He sounded less than interested and took another slow, unhurried step towards her.

Riona told herself not to panic. She told herself he was playing some sort of game. It was just a pity she didn't know the rules.

When he came to a halt before her, she resorted to an unoriginal, 'It's late. I think you should go now.'

'Probably,' he surprised her by agreeing, but made no move to leave. Instead he reached out a hand and touched her hair. 'It's a beautiful colour. Is it natural or out of a bottle?'

'I . . .' Riona was left gasping at the sheer cheek of the question.

He answered for himself, 'Natural, I'd say,' before his hand fell from her hair to her shoulder to lightly caress the skin left bare by her summer dress.

A breathless note crept into Riona's voice. 'I think you should——'

'Go . . . yes, I know.' His fingers spread to the base of her neck and felt her pulse beating a rapid tattoo. He frowned slightly. 'You're not frightened of me, are you?'

Rashly, Riona claimed, 'No, of course not!' too proud to say otherwise.

It put the smile back on the American's face, as he suggested in return, 'Then it must be love.'

'I . . . don't be absurd!' Riona was more angry now than scared.

'OK, sex, if you prefer.' He gave a low, growling laugh as he caught her hand and pressed it to his chest. 'Whichever, my heart's racing to the beat of the same drum. Feel it.'

For a moment Riona could do nothing else. She felt his heart racing as he had said, and her own beat all the harder. She snatched her hand away, only for him to clasp her by the waist.

Her eyes flew to his, in appeal, in panic. He stared back at her, no longer smiling, intent.

Desire blurred his features. She shook her head. He took no notice. Small wonder.

The first kiss. His mouth lowered to hers, infinitely slowly. She could have escaped. She didn't try. His lips on hers, a gentle caress at first, so light it was hardly felt. Oh, but enough. She betrayed herself. She opened her lips to him, opened her heart, her life.

He groaned his response, before his mouth covered hers, tasting her sweetness, desire turning to passion, demanding more, demanding all. She moaned, scared, excited. He drew her to him, close, closer, until it wasn't enough any longer, and his hands slid to her hips, lifting her body to his, forcing her to acknowledge his need of her.

Too powerful, his maleness. Too frightening to feel this way. One kiss and she wanted to...

'No...! *No*!' She twisted in his arms, pushing away from him in sudden and total rejection.

It was a second before he understood, then a look of anger and frustration crossed his handsome face. But she didn't have to struggle further. He let her go.

'I'm sorry.' Riona found herself apologising, only later asking why. 'I can't...I don't...' She shook her head.

Inarticulate mutterings, but he made something of them. The wrong thing. His dark look softened to wonder.

'Hell, I didn't realise...' His eyes searched her face and saw the panic there. 'I assumed...so few girls are these days.'

Are what? Riona could have asked, but she understood him well enough. She was just too embarrassed to say anything.

The colour was high on her cheeks, revealing, misleading, as he went on, 'I should have known. It's written all over you. I just didn't want to see it.'

Riona remained silent, but she shook her head, trying to tell him. He misread the gesture, too.

'OK, kid. It's OK.' He backed away from her, holding up his hands in truce. 'No problem. I came on too strong. It won't happen again.'

'I-I'm not . . .' a now acutely embarrassed Riona tried to explain.

He didn't give her the chance. 'You don't have to say anything. Just show me the door, huh?' he suggested with a smile that mocked himself.

He was being so nice, so reasonable that Riona felt worse. She opened her mouth, but no words came. It was easier just to do what he suggested and escort him to the door.

He left her with a wry, 'Well, it was fun while it lasted,' and a warning, 'Keep your doors locked tight, kid,' before walking off to his car.

Riona stood in the doorway, watching until he circled the car round and headed off back down the hill. She should have been relieved that he'd been put off. Should have been glad he'd deceived himself.

And she was a little, for she knew full well she couldn't handle such a man. He was too . . . too everything. Different from Fergus Ross and the other young men round Invergair. Different from anyone she'd ever met. He jangled her nerves and assaulted her pride and filled her head with such thoughts that she was on the verge of screaming.

But oh, he made her senses reel, too, and relief was nothing compared to the longing as she touched her lips and felt the imprint of his mouth still.

Treacherous senses. Insane longing.

Feelings that had to be smothered before they could leave her open to pain and disillusionment much greater than any she had ever suffered at Fergus Ross's hands.

She forced herself to remember her first and last disastrous attempt at love. To call it love, of course, was a deception in itself. Perhaps she'd thought herself in love with Fergus, but, in truth, it had just been need and fear and loneliness on her part. And on his? Sure, he had professed love until they had gone to bed together, but hadn't much bothered afterwards.

Riona hadn't complained, for her own feelings had proved insubstantial, dying even as he took her virginity with clumsy passion. The pain had barely touched her and was more bearable than the terrible emptiness in her heart. She had wanted to love Fergus, wanted to believe his promises, had slept with him rather than risk losing him. But there had been no real love there, just desire and desperation laid bare during an unloving act of intimacy. She hadn't complained when it had turned Fergus from attentive suitor to arrogant lover, because her own love had proved such a poor, false thing.

She'd just heaved an enormous sigh of relief that Fergus had to return to his ship the next day, and done her best to forget the whole sorry interlude. She'd managed fairly well, too, which said a lot about how little she had really cared for Fergus. But it had left its mark on her, making her deeply distrustful of feelings, her own or anybody else's.

Though her heart still beat painfully hard, Riona didn't put words of love to its erratic rhythm. The truth was more basic.

Cameron Adams desired her. She desired him. It was that simple. It was that dangerous. And there was no doubt what she should do. Go to any lengths to avoid him.

Only a fool would do otherwise.

CHAPTER TWO

INVERGAIR covered a large area. In theory it should have been easy to avoid him, but things weren't to work out that way.

The next day Riona cycled to the village for her groceries, and on the journey back the chain came off her bicycle. She emptied her basket and, turning the bike upside-down, began the messy job of fixing it. She was still struggling when the BMW happened along.

She saw him first, and kept her head down, but he drew to a halt and shouted from his window, 'Need a hand, kid?'

She called over her shoulder, 'No, thanks. I can manage.'

'Riona?' He frowned in surprise. He hadn't recognised her, dressed as she was in jeans and a T-shirt, with her hair tucked beneath a baseball cap.

Now he probably felt obliged to park his car on the verge and cross the road to help her.

'I really can manage,' she insisted, only to be ignored.

Crouching down by the bike, he lifted up the oily chain and took one minute flat to do what she'd been trying to for five. 'It won't stay fixed. The chain needs tightening. I'm surprised it hasn't happened before.'

It had. Four times in as many weeks. But Riona decided he didn't need to know that. He'd already made her feel incompetent enough.

'I'll take you home, just in case,' he went on, unsmiling, and, before she could protest, uprighted the bike and wheeled it towards his car.

Riona caught up with him, saying, 'You can't. You're going the other way.'

'No problem,' he dismissed. 'It should fit in the trunk.'

'Trunk?' For a moment Riona had visions of him packing her bicycle away in a box, then she caught on. 'Oh, you mean the boot.'

'No, I mean the trunk,' he drawled back. 'A boot is something you wear on your foot.'

Riona decided not to argue the point. Being an American, how could he be expected to speak proper English?

She confined herself to muttering, 'I don't think the bike will fit,' then wishing she'd kept quiet when she was proved wrong.

'You want to get in?' he suggested, after he had fetched her groceries and placed them in the boot, too.

No, Riona didn't want to get in, but she didn't want to make a fuss either. So reluctantly she climbed into the car and sat in silence while he did a three-point turn on the quiet country road, then drove back to her cottage.

The silence wasn't lost on him, as he asked point-blank, 'You sulking with me, kid?'

He made her sound childish and she claimed in response, 'Of course not!'

'Then could you possibly lighten up a little?' he continued in his almost permanently amused drawl.

It drew a not very encouraging 'Hmmph' from Riona.

Cameron Adams, however, needed no encouragement. Having reached her croft, he turned in his seat to say, 'I realise I came on a bit strong last night, but it won't happen again. So you can relax. OK?'

'OK,' Riona echoed reluctantly.

'Friends?' He offered her a hand to shake.

'Friends,' Riona agreed, and suffered his rather bone-crunching grip, before adding, 'On one condition.'

'Name it!' He smiled.

'Stop calling me "kid",' she said in all seriousness.

His smile broadened at the request and he responded easily, 'You got it, ki—honey.'

'God, no!' Riona didn't hide her distaste. '*Honey*—that's even worse.'

'All right, what should I call you? Miss Macleod?' he suggested with obvious irony.

'That'll do,' Riona answered drily, and, before he could argue the matter, climbed out of the car.

He followed, lifting her bicycle out of the boot.

'Thanks.' She forced out the word.

He shook his head at her, then left with a resigned, 'See you around, *Miss Macleod*.'

Not if I see you first, Riona thought, but didn't quite have the nerve to say. He already considered her childish enough, having lost interest in her as a woman.

She should have been pleased about that. She told herself she was. She lied.

She decided the best thing was to keep out of his way. But it really did prove impossible. The next morning, when she played organ in the village church, he was there, sitting in his great-uncle Hector's pew, in direct line of her vision. Every time she made the mistake of looking up from the music, he paused mid-song and gave her a slow, wry smile. She realised he must be laughing at her, enjoying her discomfort, well aware she didn't know how to handle him.

When the service ended and he seemed on the point of approaching her, she slipped out of the back door of the church and went overland to the doctor's house. The doctor was a non-believer who only attended church for weddings and funerals, but in Riona's eyes he was one of the most giving men in the community. Since her grandfather's death, he had insisted she join him for Sunday lunch.

The roast was prepared by his housekeeper, Mrs Ross, and sometimes the widowed lady sat down with them to enjoy it.

'Three for lunch, today,' Dr Macnab said when he'd taken off her coat and escorted her through the hall.

Riona smiled at the housekeeper as she appeared in the dining-room doorway. 'You're staying, Mrs Ross?'

'Ach, no, lass, the company's too exalted for the likes of me,' the older woman replied with a shake of the head. 'I've told the doctor. I'm away now.'

'Exalted?' Riona had a sinking feeling in the pit of her stomach.

It was the doctor who answered, 'Aye, the man himself,' and, at the ring of the doorbell, added, 'That'll be him.'

Him? Riona didn't need twenty questions. She knew. Even before she heard the doctor say, 'Come away in, Cameron, man,' and saw the American's large frame in the doorway.

He looked surprised to see her, too. Clearly the doctor hadn't warned him.

'You know Riona, of course,' Dr Macnab said, as the two exchanged stares rather than smiles.

'Miss Macleod.' The American inclined his head towards her.

She followed his lead. 'Mr Adams.'

The doctor raised a brow at such formality, but said nothing, as he led the way into the dining-room.

Though she'd lunched many times at the doctor's, Riona was the one who felt 'out of it'. While Dr Macnab and Cameron Adams chatted easily about both local and world affairs, she sat largely silent. Several times the doctor tried to draw her into the conversation, but she was completely inhibited by the American's presence.

She listened, however, and gathered that the American did not intend to sell the estate, as they'd all assumed he would.

'Initially I'll have to employ a manager to run it,' he said to the doctor. 'Apart from not having the experience, I've commitments in America.'

'So you'll be returning home soon?' Riona asked him.

'Is that wishful thinking?' he suggested drily, before saying, 'Not for a few weeks. I've managed to wangle a month's vacation from work.'

'May I ask what you do?' the doctor put in.

'I'm in construction,' Cameron Adams answered readily enough.

In construction? Riona wondered what that actually meant. Was he a bricklayer, an architect, or what? He certainly had the muscles for labouring work, but his manner implied more authority. Unless, of course, the air of authority came with his expensive clothes, which in turn came from his great-uncle Hector's money.

'You're a builder?' Riona dared to suggest.

'You could say that,' he replied, giving little away.

'What do you build?' she pursued.

He shrugged. 'Malls, mostly. The occasional cinema duplex. Condominiums, sometimes.'

'I see.' Riona absorbed this information with what she hoped was an intelligent nod. She wasn't about to admit she hadn't understood a word. Malls, duplexes and condominiums, whatever they were, weren't thick on the ground in Invergair.

'I can see I've left her deeply unimpressed,' Cameron Adams remarked to the doctor.

'Not at all,' the older man tried to make up for her lack of response. 'I'm sure it's most interesting work.'

'Fraid not, Doc,' the American laughed. 'When you've built one mall, you've built them all. So, who knows? Maybe it's time for a change.'

'You mean—move to Invergair?' Riona asked in alarm.

'Why not?' He smiled at her less than ecstatic expression. 'I am half Scotch, you know.'

'Scottish,' she echoed, not considering him such at all. 'The other's a drink.'

'I stand corrected,' he responded with an amiability that left her feeling petty.

Perhaps he was right. Perhaps she was hard to get along with.

At any rate, the doctor frowned in mild reproof before putting in, 'It's a common enough mistake. Our English counterparts often make it.'

'Well, I'll be careful not to make it again,' the American declared. 'I suspect it's going to be hard enough getting the natives to accept me. There seems to be a general opinion that I'm going to raise rents automatically, then evict those who can't pay. I guess they think, being an American, I'll be after the quick buck and nothing else.'

Riona had the grace to blush. That was exactly what she and many of the other crofters had thought. They'd certainly not envisaged him taking more than a monetary interest in his inheritance.

'Oh, I'm sure it's not personal,' Dr Macnab was quick to reassure. 'They're just worried for their future. It's not a hundred years since the last clearances, when landlords evicted tenants to make room for sheep farming.'

'So I've heard——' the American nodded '—but the people surely don't think that'll happen again? These days there must be laws to stop it.'

'Possibly,' the doctor agreed, 'only we're not talking law or logic, but a deep-rooted mistrust that's been handed down through the generations. And, with so many of the lairds being absentee landlords, attitudes have been slow to change.'

'How did they regard Sir Hector?' Cameron Adams asked, and, when the other man hesitated, added, 'You can be honest, Doc. I have no memories of my great-uncle, fond or otherwise.'

The doctor took him at his word, saying bluntly, 'Well, Sir Hector wasn't the best liked of men. He was autocratic and often downright rude to his tenants. However, he was fair about rents and, though he'd sell off any crofthouses that fell vacant, he didn't actively seek evictions.'

'Is that such a bad thing—selling off empty houses?' Cameron Adams obviously didn't view it that way.

Riona broke her silence once more. 'It is, if it's to yuppies who fancy a Highland home for three weeks of the year.'

'Aye,' Dr Macnab agreed in a less abrasive manner, 'it's a shame when there's young men forced to leave Invergair because there's no place for them to work or live.'

Cameron accepted the point with a thoughtful nod, before directing at Riona, 'Is that what happened to yours?'

'Mine?' she echoed.

'Your young man,' he continued in a drawl. 'I assume he must have had some reason to prefer going to sea than staying here with you.'

Matching his irony, Riona responded, 'Perhaps he found me hard to get along with, too.'

The American laughed, while Dr Macnab looked more uncertain. He sensed there were undercurrents he didn't understand.

'Aye, I'd say Fergus would have stayed if he could,' the doctor answered literally, 'but with two older brothers already working a not very large croft, he had little choice. If only there was something else, other than the crofting, to keep the young folk here,' he added with regret.

'Well, there must be possibilities,' the American went on. 'I'm told salmon-farming would be a good proposition, although it's not very labour-intensive. And there's the knitwear and craft industries. With a little organisation they could be real money-spinners.'

'In what way?' Riona asked, her tone deeply suspicious. Not a knitter herself, she knew many ladies who subsisted on such work. They wouldn't like any radical change.

'Well, from what I've gathered,' Cameron replied, 'a fair number of women do outwork for a knitwear factory in Glasgow. They, in turn, presumably export the hand-made garments to retail outlets who then market them at inflated prices. Now I would think it should be possible to cut out at least one if not two middlemen in the process and thereby enjoy a greater share of the profit.'

It sounded simple. Too simple. Riona looked what she felt—wholly sceptical.

It was the doctor who said, 'You mean have a label of our own. "Invergair Knitwear".'

'That's the idea, Doc.' Cameron smiled in return. 'We could get some red-hot designer up from London to make up the patterns and then it's just a question of marketing. What do you think?' he asked of Riona.

The question disconcerted her. It was easy enough to be sceptical. To come up with positive ideas was something else.

'I...I don't know much about fashion,' she finally admitted.

'Neither do I.' He shrugged it off as a problem. 'The important thing is to organise people who do and get them working for you.'

'I'm afraid I know nothing about business either,' she confessed, and realised how she must seem to him—a half-witted yokel.

The doctor chimed in, 'It's foreign territory to me, too, I have to admit, but it sounds an exciting venture. Where would you start?'

'Well, an initial step would be to hire a consultant to look into the feasibility of the project,' the American explained. 'Before that, however, I'd have to talk to the actual knitters, because if the idea isn't a runner with them it's going nowhere. My only problem is approaching them.'

Dr Macnab nodded. 'I'm afraid that *is* a problem. They're hard workers, the ladies of Invergair, and they're reliable, but they're slow on accepting new ideas, especially...'

'Especially coming from someone who's only been here five minutes,' Cameron Adams concluded for the older man, and the two laughed together.

Riona felt she had to defend her friends and neighbours. 'You can't blame them. Some of them depend entirely on knitting for their living.'

'Really?' The American was obviously surprised, but he ran on, 'In that case, all the more reason to make it a decent living. Perhaps you could help.'

'Me?' Riona echoed suspiciously.

'Yes, you could come round the area with me, introduce me to the knitters, help me to sell the idea to them.'

'I'm sorry——' she shook her head '—but it's out of the question. I'm afraid I just can't spare the time from the croft.'

'No problem,' he dismissed. 'I'll get one of the estate workers to cover for you, perhaps do some repairs while he's at it.'

'Yes, well...' Riona scrabbled around for another excuse, one he couldn't argue against.

It was Dr Macnab who put in, 'I think Riona may be hesitating because she's not completely sold on the idea herself. Is that it, lass?'

'Aye. Yes.' Riona gratefully seized on the doctor's suggestion.

She breathed a sigh of relief when Cameron Adams said, 'Fair enough.' It was somewhat premature, as he ran on, 'I can appreciate that, but I'd say it's all the more reason to come round with me.'

'You would?' Riona felt herself back on treacherous ground.

'Well, I imagine you have the knitters' interests at heart rather than mine,' he continued drily, 'and I'm sure you won't hesitate to butt in if you don't agree with me.'

'I...' Riona frowned in response. He really did make her sound a difficult character and perhaps she was, because she certainly didn't want to spend whole days in his company. 'What about Isobel...Isobel Fraser?' she suggested desperately. 'She'd be better, surely? She knows most of the knitters, too, and she's got *much* more idea of business.'

'Possibly,' Cameron conceded, 'but Isobel isn't likely to disagree with me. She's far too sweet a girl for that,' he added with a slanting smile.

Sweet! Isobel Fraser? *Sweet*? Riona almost exploded at this description. How wrong could he be? How easily he'd been taken in! If he thought Isobel Fraser sweet, then he was in real danger of ending up husband number three.

The doctor, probably thinking the same, said with gentle irony, 'Aye, you'll have no argument from Isobel.'

And Riona added in a mutter, 'Not with her eye on the main chance, anyway.'

Cameron looked quizzical. 'The main chance?'

'Never mind.' Riona shook her head, deciding against explaining that *he* was it—the main chance. Why should she be the one to spoil his illusions about Isobel?

He continued to stare at her, eyes narrowed, as if he might pursue the subject, but then Dr Macnab stepped into the rescue and asked his plans along the salmon-farming line.

Cameron relayed his intention of going to visit a couple of farms already in operation, with a view to judging the feasibility of such a scheme on Loch Gair. He confessed to knowing little about fishing of any variety, and the doctor, a keen angler, took it as an invitation to offer his knowledge and advice.

Riona fell silent again. Having entered the last conversation and ended up wishing she hadn't, she decided to adopt a low profile and hope the idea of her helping him had been dropped. She assumed it had, as, lunch over, she made her excuses and departed, expressing a positive desire to walk the three miles back to her croft. She did so with a distinct spring in her step that came from relief.

*   *   *

The relief lasted till the next morning. Seven-thirty a.m. he arrived. He and Rob Mackay, one of the estate farm workers. To say she was put in a dilemma would be untrue. Dilemma implied choice and she was given none. She was barely given time to tell Rob the jobs needing attention before Cameron Adams hustled her towards the estate Land Rover and away. He installed her into the passenger seat, then lowered the back tail-gate for Jo to jump in.

When she finally had the chance to protest, they were in motion. 'Has it occurred to you I may not want to do this?' she asked in the iciest tone she could manage.

Only to have him smile in return. 'Sure. Why do you think I got here early?'

'But what's the point?' she pursued. 'If I won't co-operate . . .'

'You'll have to——' he continued to smile '—otherwise we'll spend the day driving round and round in circles, 'cos I don't know where any of the ladies live.'

He obviously thought he had her, but Riona took a leaf from his book and shrugged. 'So? It's no skin off my nose. Rob's doing my work for the day.'

Then, having said her piece, she folded her arms and took to staring out of the window. The Land Rover provided a fine view. She felt certain she could outlast him.

He took the road to the village and parked outside the shop, where Mrs Ross and a Jean Macpherson were standing gossiping. 'Well, which way to——' he checked a list on a clipboard '—to Annie Fac-quhar-eson's?'

'Fackerson, it's pronounced,' Riona relayed with a superior air.

'Right, Fackerson. Which way?' he repeated.

Riona didn't answer. Instead she asked, 'Who compiled this list for you?'

'Isobel. Why?'

'No reason.'

'Come on,' he said at the 'I know something you don't' look on her face, 'what's wrong? Is this Annie person not one of the knitters?'

'Well, she was,' Riona conceded.

'But she's given up?' he guessed.

'You could say that,' she responded drily, before admitting, 'Old Annie Facquhareson died a month ago. It seems to have slipped Isobel's notice, unless, of course, she means young Annie.'

'That must be it,' he put in, and read off the address, 'Braeside, Ardgair.'

She nodded, 'Aye, that's young Annie's address all right. But I don't imagine she'll be doing the knitting yet. Though I might be wrong.' Riona pretended to consider the possibility. 'No, I doubt it. Five would be a bit young, don't you think?'

'Young Annie's only five?' he concluded with exasperation.

'I just said that.' Riona smiled to herself.

He grimaced, stroked out the name of Annie Facquhareson and went on to the next. 'Right, Jean Macpherson. First of all, is she dead or alive?'

'Alive,' Riona confirmed, able to see Jean Macpherson just a few yards away, still talking to Mrs Ross.

'Good. And does she knit?' he enquired drily.

She nodded, before saying, 'Yes, but——'

'I knew there'd be a but,' he cut in. 'Don't tell me. She's broken an arm? Busy sailing across the Atlantic single-handed? Emigrated to New Guinea?'

'No, she's just out at the moment,' Riona relayed.

'Out?' he repeated blankly.

'Not at home,' she said with exaggerated slowness.

His lips thinned. 'How do you know?' he asked in a manner that suggested he thought she was lying.

'Maybe I'm clairvoyant,' Riona responded unhelpfully, but her eyes betrayed her, wandering to the two women still standing gossiping.

'OK, which one is she?' he demanded.

Riona was forced to admit, 'The one in the blue dress.'

'Right, we can either go talk to her now,' he declared, 'or you can direct me to the next on the list.'

'I...' Riona hesitated. She didn't much fancy the idea of broaching the topic with Jean Macpherson in the middle of Invergair's main street and publicly advertising her association with the American, but she didn't much like giving in, either.

She was forced into action as he made to climb out of the vehicle, and she grabbed his arm to stop him. 'It'd be better if we called at her home,' she said, and, scanning the list for the easiest-going of the ladies, added, 'We could go to Betty Maclean's now. She's only a couple of miles out of the village.'

'Fine.' He nodded and, putting the vehicle in gear, followed the direction she pointed in.

A smile had reappeared on his face. It was hardly surprising. He'd won.

The smile remained on his face when she introduced him to Betty and then sat, largely silent, while he proceeded to reduce the lady to fluttering acquiescence.

They had a repeat performance in the next house and the next. Riona couldn't believe it. She'd thought his brashness would put off each and every lady. She'd thought they'd be suspicious of his grand schemes and offended by his sheer, overpowering confidence.

Instead they were carried along by his enthusiasm and bowled over by his charm. That he invited them to contribute any ideas they had to the scheme was the final seal on his popularity.

It was Riona who ended up trying to preach a little caution, and, though Cameron Adams tolerated her efforts, the women didn't want to know.

'The world's changing, Riona, lass, and we have to move with the times,' she was told by Aggie Stewart, the oldest of the knitters at seventy-four.

After that, she gave up, and limited herself to informing him how to get to each croft and providing an introduction to its inhabitant.

By the late afternoon, they'd seen about six ladies in all. It was just a fraction of the number of women capable of professional knitting in the area, but Riona felt it was enough. They were bound to relay his ideas to the rest and she told him so as they arrived back at her crofthouse.

'Possibly,' he conceded, 'but, having visited a few, I reckon I'm obliged to visit them all. Otherwise I'm going to have some offended ladies on my hands.'

Riona saw his point but said, 'Well, I can't help. I have too much to do round the croft.'

'No problem. I'll let you have Rob again,' he responded. 'You can give him a list of what's to be done, and, if he has any time over, he can do some repairs round the place.'

'No, thanks,' she refused ungraciously. 'I can do my own repairs.'

'Can you?' he challenged mildly and glanced round her back yard. The sheds were dilapidated, a door hanging from one hinge. The hen-run, now unoccupied, was more holes than fencing, and the dry stone wall was almost rubble in places.

When his eyes returned to her, Riona muttered tightly, 'I'm doing my best,' and made to climb out of the Land Rover.

He caught her arm. 'Hey, I wasn't saying otherwise. It's just too much for you, a girl on her own.'

If his manner was sympathetic, Riona was too strung up to notice. 'I can manage,' she snapped back, 'so if you're thinking of reclaiming the croft that way, you can think again.'

'What?' He was clearly taken aback by this outburst. In fact, the finest of actors couldn't have feigned his surprise.

Riona knew then she was being unfair and un-reasonable, but she couldn't stop herself. She wasn't able to behave rationally when he was around. She sent him a look that was a mixture of appeal and accusation, before wresting her arm free and jumping down from the Land Rover. Jo, the collie dog, jumped down too, but headed for the hills for his evening prowl.

Cameron caught Riona up at the house and dragged her round to face him. 'What is it with you? Do you really believe I'm out to evict you?' he demanded, angry now.

'I...' Riona's eyes went to his and any protest died on her lips. Whatever he wanted from her, it wasn't this mean little crofthouse on the hill.

They stared at each other for an endless moment, and she wanted to take back all the bad things she'd said. But no words came and finally he gave up on her, making some exasperated sound as he released his grip on her arm and wheeled round.

She watched him jump back into the Land Rover and slam hard the door and drive away without a backward glance. Tears sprang to her eyes, but she dashed them away. She had caused their quarrel. She had wanted him to leave her alone. So why should she cry about it?

CHAPTER THREE

AND why should she feel a surge of happiness when she saw the Land Rover reappear at the bottom of the hill early next day? It wasn't logical, but she didn't wait around too long analysing her emotions before tearing downstairs and out into the yard to greet him. She stopped short when she saw Rob Mackay with him.

Rob acknowledged her, 'Aye, aye,' but Cameron virtually ignored her, before the two walked round to the back of the Land Rover and began lifting out wood and wire-meshing and a collection of tools. It seemed she was going to have repairs done whether she liked it or not.

When they'd finished unloading, Rob started mending the shed door while Cameron crossed to where she stood in the doorway. Jo wagged his tail, betraying the pleasure Riona was too proud to show. Cameron patted the dog's head, but his expression remained cool as he confronted Riona. He handed her a buff-coloured envelope.

'What is it?' Riona's happiness had evaporated.

'Don't worry. It's not an eviction notice,' he responded heavily and pushed it into her hand. 'Read it carefully, before signing it.'

He turned away and Riona thought he was leaving, but instead he walked over to the dry stone wall and, to her astonishment, began to dismantle a section that badly needed rebuilding.

Riona stood for a moment, watching as he shifted stone boulders almost effortlessly, and wondered once again what he did in his other life back in America. Talking to the doctor, he sounded like an educated man with sophisticated ideas and an executive air. Labouring in her back yard, he could pass for a construction site

47

worker who wasn't afraid of getting his hands dirty. Which was the real Cameron Adams?

Whichever, he was now the laird and, as such, far out of her reach. If Riona needed a reminder of the fact, it was in her hand—in the shape of a buff-coloured envelope. She carried it inside and, sitting down at the kitchen table, turned it over and over in her hand. The easygoing Cameron of yesterday hadn't given her this; her landlord had. He'd tried to be friendly, and she'd been churlish in response. Whatever was in the envelope, she very probably deserved it.

She was wrong. She didn't. She twice read the document inside, looking for a catch and finding none. It was an agreement, offering her lifetime tenancy of the croft, rent to remain currently static, future increases to be limited to inflation rate and unaffected by any improvements the estate might make to the property. It was on a standard form with handwritten additions witnessed by Agatha Mackenzie and Morag Mackinnon, housekeeper and housemaid at Invergair Hall. It gave her total security and cost her nothing and was more generous than she had any right to expect after her surly behaviour.

It was some time before she went out to him. She rehearsed a speech of gratitude and apology, but it became a confused mess in her head the instant she came near him.

He didn't notice her at first. He was working steadily, stripped down to the waist in the bright June sunshine. He was tanned an even brown, suggesting he was accustomed to working outside.

Riona stopped short, her eyes drawn to his broad, muscular back and the rivulets of sweat running down it. Her breath caught and she wondered if a man could be described as beautiful. If he could, Cameron Adams was.

He must have sensed her presence. He straightened and turned suddenly, and she blushed, as if guilty of something.

He nodded towards the envelope in her hand. 'Have you signed it?'

'I—er—no, it's all right,' she garbled out. 'There's no need. I was being silly...yesterday, I mean. I realise you don't want to evict me.'

'You do?' He sounded suspicious at her almost humble tone.

She nodded. 'I suppose I was just being...well, as you say—hard to get along with,' she admitted, pulling a face.

He raised a surprised brow at what was clearly intended as an apology, then conceded generously, 'I don't know, maybe it was my fault, too. When I get an idea, I tend to expect other people to go along with it. I guess I'm not used to hard-headed Scots girls with minds of their own.'

A smile made the last a compliment, and Riona smiled back, but it was an automatic response. Their eyes conveyed more as they met and held and admitted the reality of their feelings.

It was a physical thing, not a simple pull of attraction, but a great big wrench. The way he looked at her made her stomach knot and her heart race and her head light, and instinctively she wanted to fight with him all over again. She wanted to fight with him because it seemed by far the safest thing to do.

'So this time I'm asking,' he said, eyes still holding hers, 'will you please come along and introduce me to the other ladies this afternoon?'

He made it easy for her. She just had to say no. Say no and he wouldn't bother her again.

'I...yes, OK,' she said in a rush, suddenly tired of being sane and sensible and safe.

He didn't hide his satisfaction. He'd got his way, as he probably had a thousand times before with other women he left breathless in his wake.

'Actually, no, when I think——' she tried to back out of it.

He wouldn't let her. 'Uh-huh! Don't think. Much better go with your instincts.'

'I...' Riona opened her mouth to argue, but couldn't think of an excuse that wouldn't sound lame.

And he continued quickly, 'Well, I'd better finish the job I've started.' He indicated the section of wall he was rebuilding.

To Riona, what he'd already done looked impressive. 'Is that what you do for a living? Actual building, I mean?'

The question seemed to amuse him, as he said, 'There's not much call for dry stone walls in downtown Boston, but yes, you could say I'm in the same line of work.'

'As a foreman?' Riona was almost positive he wasn't an ordinary labourer.

'Of sorts,' he confirmed. 'Why? Were you hoping for something grander?'

'No, of course not!' Riona denied sharply. 'It doesn't matter to me what you do. Why should it?'

'No reason.' He ignored her disgruntled look and smiled to himself before ending the conversation with, 'So I'll see you later.'

It wasn't a question but a statement, as he turned back to the wall and continued the task in hand. Realising she'd been dismissed, Riona headed towards the croft-house, then changed her mind and, whistling the collie, took to the hills. She climbed as far as her main flock of sheep and moved them to an adjoining field to graze. It didn't take her long. At sixteen, Jo was getting old, but he was still an excellent sheep-dog. Trained by her grandfather, he needed the minimum of instruction.

Riona, however, was in no hurry to return to the croft, and sat down on one of the large stones that were scattered across the hillside. From that vantage-point she could see her yard. Cameron Adams had abandoned his wall-building temporarily to help Rob erect new fencing round the chicken-run. She was too far away to hear what they were saying, but clearly they were at ease with each other. It seemed the new laird didn't expect the deference Sir Hector had always demanded of his estate workers.

But he was still laird, Riona reminded herself of the fact. He might just be a construction worker in the United States. He might have had as limited an education as herself. He might come from as humble a background. But in Scotland his lairdship put him in a social category way above her own.

She might tell herself that she was as good as Cameron Adams any day of the week. She might even believe it. But that wouldn't make any difference. She was never going to be regarded as suitable.

Suitable for what? Riona's lips twisted as she recognised the very absurdity of her thoughts. Cameron wasn't worrying about whether she was 'suitable' or not. He'd probably never even considered that. He was simply attracted to her on a sexual level. She knew that. She wasn't a fool, and besides, he'd made it obvious.

And herself? Riona questioned as she gazed back down the hill at him. Still stripped to the waist, he had returned to reconstructing the wall. Even at a distance she felt the power of his attraction, and her body stirred with unfamiliar desire. He worked effortlessly, with strong, easy movements. He would make love the same way. Riona knew enough to know that, but then she wasn't quite the innocent he imagined.

Her thoughts went once more to Fergus and their brief relationship. She had known him since childhood. They had gone to the same school, although he had been a couple of classes ahead of her. Red-headed and good-looking, he had been popular with the girls and had known it. Riona had been one of the few to resist his charm, which was probably why he kept pursuing her in between other romances.

He had eventually gone away to the Navy, but had returned, at Christmas-time, for six weeks' leave. Riona, torn between running the croft and nursing her ailing grandfather, had been oblivious of the festive season. When Fergus had appeared to offer a hand, it had seemed a godsend. If she had been less tired or less sad—for her grandfather was dying slowly before her eyes—Riona would have asked herself what Fergus wanted in return.

Her grandfather had died a month after Christmas. She had got through the funeral somehow, but her grief had been terrible. Salvation had come through work. January snowstorms had hit a couple of days later and the sheep had to be rescued from the hill. Fergus had worked by her side through three exhausting days, the last days of his leave.

It had hardly been a romantic setting, dragging buried, sometimes dead sheep out of thigh-high drifts of snow, but it had both weakened and heightened emotions. Bitterly cold, desperately unhappy, she had turned to Fergus, seeking love, comfort, a cure for grief.

She didn't blame Fergus for taking advantage. She was the one who had deceived herself by calling her dependence on him love. She was the one who had wanted to believe, however briefly, in Fergus's claims of undying devotion, rather than remind herself of all the other girls who had doubtless heard the same words from him.

And afterwards, when intimacy had destroyed even that illusion of love, she had felt too low to object to Fergus's subsequent attitude. No 'I love you's then. Instead she had glimpsed the old Fergus, visibly preening himself and openly boasting that he'd always known he'd get her one day. She'd said nothing, willing him gone. He'd promised to write, and she'd been relieved he hadn't. She just wanted to forget how weak and foolish she'd been.

Perhaps she'd forgotten too well—for there she was again, accepting another man's help round the croft and wondering what the cost was going to be. She looked down at Cameron Adams once more and forced herself to face facts. He wasn't spending a morning mending a dry stone dike for the good of his health. He wasn't offering a new tenancy agreement because he hoped to be declared Landlord of the Year.

The truth was he wanted her the same way as Fergus had, and afterwards he would walk away just as easily. The only difference was her feelings for the American weren't some pathetic mixture of gratitude and guilt. They were much more powerful and dangerous—and only a fool would ignore the warning bell that rang in her head every time he was near.

Riona went back down the hill, determined to withstand the American's considerable charm. She made lunch for him and Rob, then remained cool and remote during the meal.

She kept this distance when they drove round the knitters' cottages, but either he didn't notice or didn't care. He used his charm on the older ladies as he discussed ideas for a knitwear label, and clearly left them all awed by his magnetic personality.

Riona didn't blame them. He was hard to resist. She watched his mouth curve into a lazy smile and her heart literally skipped a beat. She listened to his deep, drawling voice, and it sent a shiver down her spine. She sensed his genuine warmth towards the simple folk of Invergair, yet recognised his own sophistication. And, all the time, she had to remind herself that he wasn't for her.

Was she already in love with him then? Later Riona felt that maybe she had been. But she went on denying it, went on being hard to get along with, in the hope that it would save her.

Perhaps Cameron had understood that her resistance was all put on, for her coolness did not put him off. He dropped her back at the cottage, without making any further arrangements to see her, then quite simply turned up next morning in the hired BMW with Rob.

Riona felt once more that surge of happiness that he had come back. It was absurd when she tried so hard to send him away.

'I've arranged to see a salmon-farm near Gairloch,' he said, when Rob disappeared towards the out-buildings. 'I'm not sure of the way. I wondered if you'd come as my guide.'

No. That was all she had to say. Then he'd get back in the Land Rover and drive off. But Riona didn't want to say no. She wanted just one more day, a day she wouldn't spoil by being sullen, a day she could enjoy, before she finally put a break on any friendship with the American.

She nodded her head, then, indicating her cut-down jeans and granny-style T-shirt, said, 'Should I change?'

'No, you're fine,' he replied, his eyes on her face, not her clothes.

He himself was dressed in denims and a casual white shirt, but it wasn't the same. His clothes whispered money, while hers betrayed a lack of it. But he didn't seem to care, taking her arm before she could change her mind, and installing her into the passenger seat of the BMW.

Having made a decision to give herself this day, Riona became a different girl. They drove with the windows down and a cooling breeze fanned their faces as he talked of the fish-farms he planned and she forgot for a while that he was laird and she just tenant. She allowed herself to smile and laugh and betray a nature as bright and lovely as her looks.

They arrived at their destination late morning and, after a tour round a rather poorly run salmon-farm, began the journey home. Riona didn't question the fact that he had asked no directions of her. Nor did she question his announcement that they would stop for lunch on the way home, until they pulled off the road and parked above a sandy inlet on the shores of Loch Gair.

'There's no place to eat round here,' she said, thinking he meant them to walk to the nearest hotel.

'That's all right. Mrs Mackenzie has prepared a picnic,' he explained, then climbed out to take the hamper the housekeeper had packed from the boot of the car.

He carried it down the slope and Riona trailed after him, slipping off her sandals as they reached the beach. It was a beautiful day, the noon sun high in the sky and reflecting off the crystal-clear waters of the loch. It was a perfect place for a picnic, seated on the soft sand, the silence broken only by the gentle lapping of water on the shore.

Yet suddenly Riona felt as nervous as a kitten. Kneeling on the edge of the travelling rug he'd brought, she watched him unpack the food and uncork the wine, then shook her head when he offered her a glass.

'I don't drink,' she said quite truthfully.

'What, never?' He lifted what might have been a mocking brow.

She found herself reacting primly, saying, 'My grandfather thought alcohol dulled the mind, deadened the conscience and destroyed the soul.'

'Really!' Cameron tried and failed to hide a smile at this rather extreme pronouncement. 'I take it your grandfather was a religious man.'

'Not at all,' Riona denied flatly. 'He thought religion a crutch for the weak and an excuse for the righteous.'

An eyebrow rose again. 'Your grandfather was certainly a man of strong opinions.'

There was no criticism in Cameron's tone, but Riona still felt defensive. She had loved her grandfather, even if others had thought him cantankerous and self-opinionated. He had cared for her in his own way, although affection had always been brief in expression and gesture, and he had taught her to be self-contained and strong. Given the choice of going to the Royal

College of Music in Edinburgh or staying to take care
of her grandfather, she had had no doubts. She owed
him everything—including her musical talent.

'Maybe, but he respected other people's opinions, too,'
she declared, her admiration of her grandfather un-
dimmed by his passing.

'Which, from all accounts, puts him one up on my
great-uncle, Sir Hector,' Cameron commented in response, then asked, 'Did they ever meet, the two of
them?'

'Oh, yes.' She pulled a face at the memory.

'So who won?' he asked astutely.

Riona smiled. 'I'd say it was about a draw. Sir Hector
had a house party of guests up from London one time,
and he decided to hold a ceilidh in the Hall. He expected
my grandfather, Roddy, and his friends to play at it for
free. Well, my grandfather told him he'd play organ at
his funeral for free, but nowhere else, and Sir Hector
almost had a fit, then and there.'

'But did he pay?' Cameron smiled back.

'Oh, aye, sixty pounds. After all, he couldn't do much
else,' Riona pointed out, 'having promised all his friends
a real Scottish night.'

'That doesn't sound like a draw, more like a total
victory for your grandfather,' Cameron judged
admiringly.

Riona shook her head. 'No, Sir Hector got his own
back. You see, the next few years he sent the builders
in for repairs to the estate houses; somehow our cottage
was missed out.'

'That's why it's in such a state,' Cameron concluded,
frowning. 'And is that why you resent me helping?
Because I'm Sir Hector's great-nephew?'

Riona shrugged. It wasn't that simple, but she had no
inclination to explain the mixed feelings she had towards
him.

He didn't press her, and instead turned to the picnic
hamper. He handed her a plate and left her to help

herself. With a good appetite, Riona took as much as she thought she'd eat.

He smiled in approval. 'It makes a real change to be with a woman who isn't watching her weight all the time.'

For a moment Riona felt ridiculously pleased at being regarded as a woman, then sobered as she wondered if his remark was actually a veiled insult. Perhaps he was suggesting she *should* be watching her weight?

'I suppose most of your girlfriends are much slimmer—like fashion models you see in magazines,' she finally responded.

But if he heard the disdain in her voice, he still smiled, before saying, 'Why do you assume I have girlfriends in the plural?'

'I...' Riona frowned at the question. He was right. She had assumed it. 'I don't know. I just imagined you would have, since you're still single.'

'Safety in numbers?' he joked, before confirming, 'Yes, well, I have to admit you're right. As a thirty-five-year-old bachelor, I've inevitably dated a few women in my time. I guess you could describe me as a serial monogamist.'

'A what?' she echoed blankly.

'A serial monogamist,' he repeated. 'That means I date one woman after the other, but only one at a time.'

'Oh.' Riona wasn't sure how to take this, but a slanting smile told her he was enjoying disconcerting her.

She decided it was time to drop the subject of his love life and turned her attention back to the food on her plate. She'd helped herself to cold chicken and green salad and it was very tasty, but the heat made her throat dry and she longed for a drink.

He saw her looking enviously at the wine he was sipping and poured her a glass. 'Here. This stuff can hardly be classified as alcohol.'

She took the wine offered and tentatively sniffed it before putting it to her lips. It smelled neither sour like beer nor strong like whisky. Instead it sparkled like crystal and smelled of sunshine and danced like bubbles on her tongue. It was Riona's first glass of French champagne and it tasted absolutely delicious.

'Like it?' Cameron smiled at her expression.

She nodded. 'It's like lemonade for grown-ups,' she said impulsively and made him laugh.

'That's exactly what it is,' he agreed, pouring himself another glass.

Thirsty, Riona finished her own drink, and he topped up her glass, at the same time warning, 'Only it isn't, so I wouldn't drink too quickly.'

'But it's not really alcohol,' Riona reminded him what he'd said, and he made a slight face.

'Well, yes and no,' he said, retracting his earlier statement as he advised, 'You could still get mildly drunk on it.'

Riona pulled a face in return. She didn't feel drunk, not even mildly. She just felt good, and when she finished the second glass she felt better. She held out her glass for a refill.

He hesitated for a fraction, but, when she gave him a wide, happy smile, he emptied the bottle into her glass.

Riona talked a good bit after that. She asked him about his parents, and he told her that his mother—who had been Sir Hector's niece—had died of cancer when he was eight. His father had remarried when he was thirteen.

'Did you like your stepmother?' she asked with the point-blank curiosity of someone who was vaguely drunk but didn't know it.

He raised a brow at the question, then shook his head. 'Not so you'd notice. I called her the dragon lady.'

'Behind her back?' she quizzed.

'No, to her face,' he admitted, and they both laughed together.

'So, have you brothers or sisters?' Riona continued her inquisition.

He shrugged. 'A stepsister, Melissa.'

'Younger or older?'

'Younger by ten years.'

Riona wasn't too drunk to calculate that Melissa was currently twenty-five. She was drunk enough, however, for illogical remarks like, 'I suppose she has a model-girl figure.'

He looked surprised, then amused in conceding, 'As a matter of fact, yes, Mel is pretty slim.'

'I suppose she's beautiful, too,' Riona added, suddenly feeling very sorry for herself.

'Sensational,' he agreed, laughter in his voice. 'Why do you ask?'

'No reason,' Riona claimed, feeling quite an irrational dislike for a girl she'd never met. 'Is she clever?'

'A graduate of Vassar,' Cameron stated, leaving Riona to guess that was really something. 'In fact, I have to admit it: she's so damn near perfect, it's been impossible for her to find a man to match up,' he added, a smile reaching his eyes as he looked at Riona.

She took it the smile was for Miss Perfection, his stepsister, and found herself saying outright, 'If she's that perfect, it's a wonder you don't volunteer for the part. After all, she isn't your real sister, is she?'

'No, she isn't,' he agreed, 'and, yes, it has been suggested that Melissa and I would make an ideal couple.'

Suggested by whom? Riona wondered, but didn't ask. She was already wishing she hadn't been quite so nosy. She'd known there would be women in his life. Did she really need to know their names or hear how perfect they were?

She closed the subject herself with an abrupt, 'Well, I think I'll go for a walk,' and got to her feet. She swayed slightly and was surprised by how light her head felt.

'I think I'll go with you,' Cameron announced with another smile, and followed her up.

Riona wanted to argue, but she couldn't summon the energy necessary, and he was already taking her hand and leading the way along the beach.

With other men Riona was aware of her own size and height—five feet nine in bare feet. With Cameron Adams, she was aware of his. Her head just reached his chin. Her hand disappeared in his. He made her feel very feminine and oddly vulnerable.

They walked in silence along the sand until the beach ended at a rock face, then turned to look at the water lapping their feet and the hills rising from the opposite shore, ablaze with yellow broom and purple heather.

'Is there anywhere else so beautiful?' Cameron wondered aloud, before switching his eyes from the view to her.

'I don't know,' Riona admitted. 'I've only ever lived in the Highlands.'

'And you've never thought of leaving? For college or for work?' he asked, frowning a little.

Riona supposed she could have told him about the Royal College of Music, but she wasn't sure if he'd believe her. He'd only ever heard her playing Scottish reel music.

'It wasn't possible,' she finally said, and unconsciously her face clouded over.

'Because of your grandfather,' Cameron concluded. 'Dr Hamish said you'd nursed him to the last. It must have been hard.'

Riona shook her head, denying it. 'I loved him,' she said simply, and turned from him.

He caught her arm and gently pulled her round again. He saw a suspicion of tears in her beautiful green eyes. 'I didn't mean to upset you.'

'You haven't,' she claimed, even as a tear slid silently down her cheek.

He put out a long finger and stemmed it. She bowed her head and shut her eyes to prevent any more. She felt silly. She didn't normally cry so easily, didn't normally cry at all.

He took her chin and tilted her face to his once more. She tried to look tough, but her bottom lip trembled at

the compassion in his eyes. She tried to look away and
his hand cupped her cheek.

'You can cry with me,' he said, his hand softly
touching her skin, sliding to her hair.

Riona felt his pity, but didn't want it. She resented it
and him, even as every sense cried out with a different
need. Her lips parted in protest, but the words caught
in her throat as he lifted his other hand to cradle her
head.

It suddenly seemed hard to breathe. She licked her
dry lips, unconsciously provocative, and his eyes followed the movement, then his fingers. He traced her
mouth, watching her face as he did so. He slowly bent
his head, giving her every chance to escape.

And, even as her mind said, I mustn't let him, her
heart beat a different message. His lips touched hers,
gentle at first, no more than a healing breath on her
soft, child's mouth. Perhaps that was all he would have
done—kissed her with tenderness—if her mouth hadn't
slowly opened to him like a flower, seeking more than
the coolness of his breath, wanting the taste of him, warm
and moist on her tongue.

She lifted her face to his, and was lost. He clasped
her closer and, groaning his acceptance, covered her lips
with his. He kissed her with a rough sensuality that made
her want more, and her arms went round his neck, and
her hands held his head, dragging it to her own.

He kissed her over and over, but it wasn't enough to
satisfy the need in her. She fell with him on to the sand,
and they lay on their sides, still kissing. Then he rolled
her on to her back, a hard leg trapping hers, and his
mouth left hers to trail downwards. Skilled fingers undid
the top buttons of her T-shirt and pushed aside the flimsy
bra she wore, and she tensed for their touch. She did
not expect the shock of pleasure as his mouth, not his
hand, covered the peak of her breast and began to play
and suck and tease on her already hardened nipple. Such

shock that she arched to him. Such pleasure that she moaned for him. And was lost.

He could have made love to her then and there, on that lonely beach. Riona was incapable of stopping him. It was a hard truth to face. But it was he who stopped himself, he who drew away from her eventually and looked briefly at her full, beautiful breasts, before drawing the sides of her T-shirt together.

It was a wretched feeling, rejection. But that had to be faced, too, as he sat up and away from her, and stared out towards the loch.

She barely heard his mutter of, 'I want you, but not like this,' and it didn't lessen her feelings of humiliation, as she buttoned up her T-shirt. She should have been the one to call a halt. She should never have let him kiss her, never let him pull her down on the sand, never let…

Angry with herself, angry with him, she scrambled to her feet and left him sitting there. When he called out her name, she kept walking. He followed, shadowing her until they reached the picnic things. She bent to collect her sandals and would have walked away again, if he hadn't caught at her arm.

She refused to look at him. He sighed heavily, then said, 'I took advantage. I'm sorry.'

It wasn't what Riona had expected and she turned to him in surprise.

'The champagne made you a little tipsy. I knew that,' he went on to admit. 'I shouldn't have made a pass at you.'

Riona stopped feeling angry, and started feeling guilty. She supposed she had been light-headed and her guard down.

'I didn't exactly fight you off,' she admitted in turn, shamefaced.

He smiled, 'No, you were delightful, but how much was the champagne and how much was me is the question.'

Riona blushed at the 'delightful', and decided it was a question best left unanswered. She should just be grateful he had overestimated her intoxication.

He smiled again, at the pink colour in her cheeks, then, releasing her arm, bent to pack away the picnic things. Riona felt awkward just standing there, and bent to help him.

They drove home, not friends exactly, but not in silence, either. Cameron talked of his plans for converting Invergair Hall from a mausoleum, as he put it, to what sounded like a luxury home, without destroying the essential character of the house. Riona, who had visited the Hall a few times as a girl, agreed it was presently a draughty barn of a place, and didn't disagree with the idea of improvements. She just wasn't sure how she felt about him living there permanently.

It would have been so easy to dream, so easy to let herself imagine Cameron was interested in her, beyond a brief affair.

But, in real life, men like Cameron had too many girls interested in them to be interested in only one. Even if he hadn't been laird and heir to Sir Hector's wealth, he would still have had his pick of the women.

Men like Cameron fooled around until they were forty, then married someone to give them children. Only the someone wouldn't be anyone like Riona. Why should it be, when there were any number of daughters of minor aristocracy who would overlook his Americanness to acquire an ancient Scottish seat? Riona could never compete with the Lady Sarahs and the Lady Carolines, with their correct accents and their polished manners and their beautiful clothes. She would be a fool even to try.

By the time they returned to the croft, the effect of the champagne had worn off and Riona was back to being hard to get along with.

When Cameron turned in his seat and, smiling, said, 'About tomorrow——' she cut him off abruptly.

'I won't be able to help you. I have to go to Inverness.'

'Say, that's a coincidence.' His smile broadened. 'You'll never guess where I'm going tomorrow.'

Riona had a feeling she could guess. She hoped she was wrong.

She wasn't.

He went on, 'To see another fish-farm just outside Inverness.'

'Really.' Riona still hoped she was flattering herself—and that he was not about to offer her a lift.

But she was right again, as he continued, 'So what time should I pick you up?'

'It's OK. You don't have to bother,' she said quickly. 'I can easily get the bus.'

'That's crazy,' he dismissed. 'I'm driving to Inverness, anyway. Why not come with me?'

'I...I get car sick,' she garbled out, and it sounded what it was—a feeble excuse. 'On long journeys,' she added, recalling she'd spent much of the last few days travelling around with him.

'So?' He shrugged. 'If you get car sick, you must get bus sick, too. I'll come equipped with a plastic bag.'

'No, really. It's all right. I...' She searched frantically for another excuse.

'Don't want to go with me,' he supplied, a wry look on his face. 'Yes, I've got the message. The question is why?'

'I—I...' His directness threw her.

'I won't expect you to sleep with me in repayment, you know,' he stated in an offhand drawl.

Riona's face flared with colour. Did he have to be so crude?

'I didn't think...' she started to protest.

'Didn't you?' He pulled a slight face. 'After the way I acted on the beach, I guess my motives are suspect. However, you have my word: if you come to Inverness with me, I'll keep my hands to myself and stick to strictly impersonal topics, like the weather... So what time should I pick you up?'

Riona opened and shut her mouth. He was irrepressible.

'Nine o'clock,' he suggested.

And she took the easy way out, agreeing, 'Nine o'clock.'

Her capitulation must have seemed suspiciously sudden, but a slight frown was quickly replaced by a smile of satisfaction.

Cameron Adams was used to getting his own way, Riona imagined. One look from those dark blue eyes, the flash of a wicked smile, and women were brought to their knees. Silly, susceptible women—there were enough of them in the world.

Riona refused to be one.

CHAPTER FOUR

NINE, Riona had agreed, and by half-past eight she was standing outside the village store, waiting for the bus. She wasn't alone. There was old Donald MacIver, travelling to Inverness to see his daughter, and Betty Maclean, making a once-a-month trip to the chiropodist's.

She was just thinking she was home free when the BMW appeared from the other direction. She quickly turned her back, while Betty started to say, 'Isn't that himself? Why, he's slowing down.'

Riona's heart sank. She assumed it was bad luck he'd come this way and spotted her, but it seemed not, as he drew to a halt beside her, and stepped out of the car. 'Thought I'd catch you here. We must have got our times mixed up.'

Of course he knew they hadn't. He was speaking for their audience's benefit, while his eyes flashed her another message, telling her she'd been outmanoeuvred.

Riona might have argued, but he didn't give her a chance, turning to say to the rest, 'Are you waiting for the bus, too?'

Donald gave a nod that suggested he would have doffed his cap had he been wearing one, while Betty beamed at him, saying 'Aye, your lairdship,' in a suitably sycophantic manner.

Riona just gritted her teeth.

The American looked amused, as he invited them all to, 'Climb on board.'

Betty hesitated, flustered by the idea of travelling in the laird's car, but he opened the rear door and ushered her and Donald inside.

That left Riona. Having shut in the rest of his passengers, he opened the front door for her. She stood where she was.

'Come on,' he said in an undertone, 'surely I'm safe enough now.'

'What do you mean?' She frowned back.

'I've got you two chaperons.' He nodded towards Betty and Donald in the back of the car.

Riona gritted her teeth once more at his gentle mockery, but, when he caught hold of her arm to press-gang her into the car, she put up no resistance. She was too conscious of Betty in the back; Betty's nickname round Invergair was Betty the News. Riona didn't want to give her anything juicy to report.

The car journey took a little over an hour. Riona found every minute a strain; not so the rest. Cameron Adams soon put Betty at her ease and she gossiped most of the journey, while Donald clearly enjoyed speeding along in the BMW. When they arrived in Inverness, the American delivered them to their destination.

'How to win friends and influence people,' Riona muttered rather sourly, as they drew away from a broadly smiling Betty outside the chiropodist's.

'What's wrong with that?' he challenged. 'If I do move to Invergair, it will make life a lot easier, being accepted by the locals.'

'Well, I think you've made a convert in Betty... *your lairdship*.' She mimicked the other woman's frequently used address to him.

He laughed, before drawling back, 'You know us Americans. We just *love* titles.'

He'd obviously read her thoughts and was making fun of her. She lapsed into silence once more until they reached the town centre, then she announced crisply, 'You can drop me here.'

'Why? Where are you going?' he asked, pulling into a parking space.

Riona decided it was none of his business, and said, 'Nowhere in particular.'

'You're just going shopping,' he concluded for himself. 'That seems a fairly universal occupation among women.'

The comment annoyed Riona greatly. 'As a matter of fact, I haven't come shopping. I never come shopping. I'm here to work,' she informed him in cool tones.

'To work?' His brows raised. 'At what?'

He made it sound as if he imagined her incapable of anything but herding sheep, and she snapped, 'I give piano lessons.'

'You don't say!' He looked a shade more impressed. 'At a school, you mean?'

'No, I teach people in their own homes,' she relayed.

He frowned. 'Well, I hope your clients are all female.'

'Why?' Riona frowned at his tone.

'You can't be that naïve, surely?' He slanted his head on one side and let his eyes wander from her face to her body, its curvaceousness still apparent in a plain white blouse and cotton skirt.

Riona understood then what was meant by bedroom eyes. 'Not every man sees a woman as a...as a...'

'Sex object?' he suggested at her reluctance to say the words. 'Possibly not, but I'd say most men would find you attractive. And that touch-me-not manner of yours isn't going to stop them. In fact, some might consider it a positive turn-on.'

Riona didn't believe him. He was just trying to embarrass her. He was succeeding, too, as she felt the colour rising in her cheeks.

He seemed oblivious, asking outright, 'So, are any of your pupils male?'

'Yes, one.'

'Young or old?'

'Young.'

He shook his head in disapproval. 'And you go to this guy's house?'

'I don't have much alternative. That's where the piano is,' she pointed out.

'Do you take any protection?' he pursued.

'What do you suggest?' she countered drily. 'A switchblade? A revolver? Or maybe a machine gun? This isn't America, you know,' she added in a tone that said she was very glad it wasn't.

'There are alternatives,' he said impatiently. 'Some women carry around mace to spray in an attacker's eyes.'

'Really?' She continued to play him along for a moment, before saying, 'Well, somehow I don't think that would go down very well with his mother.'

'His mother?' Cameron Adams repeated with a frown.

'Yes, didn't I say?' She feigned innocence. 'Little Ewan, my one male client, is only seven. Or might he be eight? I seem to remember he had a birth——'

'All right, all right,' he cut in, 'I was just looking out for your interests, though God knows why!'

Riona's lips thinned at his exasperated tone. She hadn't asked for his patronage and she certainly didn't need it. She gathered the holdall at her feet and, with a vague nod of farewell, made to open the passenger door.

He caught her arm, saying, 'So what time do I pick you up and where?'

She shook her head. 'I'll be staying overnight.' She indicated the bag she was clutching.

'Staying where?' he immediately quizzed.

She frowned at his curiosity, but told him, 'In a bed and breakfast along the river. I always stay there.'

'How about dinner, then?' he added, taking her by surprise.

'I thought you were going back to Invergair?'

'There's no rush. I can drive home afterwards... So what do you think? I'm told the Royal Caledonian serves a good dinner.'

'*No, not there!*' Riona was plainly horrified by his choice.

His eyes narrowed at her reaction. 'Why? Is there something wrong with the place?'

'I...no...I should have said,' she went on hastily, 'I can't have dinner anywhere. I'll be working, you see.'

'Working?' His brows lifted. 'At night, too?'

'Well, yes,' she confirmed shortly.

'Teaching piano?' he pursued.

'I...that sort of thing,' she hedged the real answer.

He looked suspicious, then asked with his usual directness, 'You're not seeing some man, are you?... Because if so, you don't have to lie about it. I'm not going to advertise the fact around Invergair.'

'No, I am not,' Riona ground back. 'Though it's hardly any of your business if I were, *Mr Adams*.'

'Perhaps not,' he conceded, 'but I think poor old Angus might have something to say about it.'

'Angus?' she repeated blankly.

'The boyfriend,' he reminded her.

'His name is Fergus,' she corrected, temper rising, 'and, as you don't even know him, I don't see why you should be concerned over his feelings.'

'Call it sympathy for a fellow sufferer,' he drawled in response.

Riona didn't believe a word, but couldn't resist pointing out, 'Well, accepting Fergus would be jealous of me seeing another man, I can't think he'd be too keen on me going to dinner with you.'

'True,' he granted with a shrug, then went on infuriatingly, 'Is that why you won't come to dinner with me? You're frightened of upsetting the boyfriend?'

'No!' she burst out in exasperation. 'I've told you. I'm working.'

'I know what you told me,' he drawled back, 'I just feel you're hiding something. The question is what.'

The nerve of him had Riona seething, but the accuracy of his suspicions kept her silent. She was hiding something. Nothing particularly bad, but nothing she wanted him to know either.

'Look, I have to go. Thanks for the lift.' She jerked her arm out of his grip and scrambled out of the car.

He followed, a second or two later, but by then she'd nipped into the nearest shop, Melven's bookstore, and, disappearing into a crowd of tourists, exited by the back door. She thought she heard him call her name, and picked up speed, running the length of the alley, before turning left, followed by an immediate right, almost losing herself as well as him in the process.

It was all very silly and dramatic, she thought later. She should just have admitted what she spent the evening doing.

She'd started teaching piano shortly after her grandfather's death, and had obtained the night-time job through one of her pupils, Mary Mathieson. The girl's father managed the Royal Caledonian, the hotel where Cameron Adams had suggested they dine. It was one of the largest hotels in Inverness, with various public rooms, including a cocktail lounge that boasted a resident piano player. The latter had his evening off on a Thursday and that was where Riona came in. Between the hours of eight and midnight, she provided background music in this bar.

At first, she'd been nervous, but she'd soon realised few of the customers listened very closely or noticed her, tucked away in a far corner. She didn't much care for the bland music she had to play, but it paid well enough and helped repay debts incurred during her grandfather's illness.

It was a busy day for her. Though she enjoyed giving the piano lessons, there were fairly lengthy walks between each appointment, and it was almost seven before she arrived at her boarding house. The owner was a friend of the Mathiesons and always kept a small back room for Riona to use mid-week. She also allowed Riona to leave her 'performing dresses' there. One was a black evening affair, with bootlace straps, a tight bodice and flaring skirt coming to a respectable knee-line. The other was a white version of the same. Riona felt neither dress was really her, but she'd bought them cheap in a sale in a posh dress shop, and topped them with an old waterproof to walk the short distance to the Royal Caledonian.

She left the coat at Reception, then went to the cocktail bar; it was virtually empty, as most guests were still at dinner.

'Hello, love,' the head barman, Eric, greeted her familiarly, 'come to entertain the masses?'

'Not quite.' Riona scanned the bar and counted six people altogether: two customers, Eric and the three waiters who worked under him.

'It'll hot up later, I expect. Yesterday we were packed out—a crowd of Americans. Talk about brash!' Eric wrinkled his nose. 'All Harvey Wallbangers and vodka martinis. Still, they know how to tip.'

Riona shook her head at him. She didn't think it fair to make such a sweeping generalisation. Most American tourists she'd met had been warm, friendly and genuinely appreciative of the beauty of the Scottish Highlands. If people like Eric called them brash, it was often through envy of their sheer confidence in life.

Riona's thoughts strayed to Cameron Adams as she considered how the reality of him had turned out to be so different from the crofters' imaginings. When they'd first heard the estate had not been left to the most likely candidate—a second cousin who occasionally travelled up from England—but to an American great-nephew of whom they knew nothing, the general reaction had been consternation.

They had pictured this JR-like stranger parcelling up the land, then auctioning it off by proxy. No one had thought for a moment he would arrive in person, like a breath of fresh air, with plans to regenerate the estate-plans that the old laird would never even have contemplated.

So why was *she* being so hostile to him? Was she an Eric, too—envious of his confidence, his vitality? She hoped not. She was disconcerted, yes. And confused. And intimidated. All of them and more, she admitted, as the image of his dark, handsome head sent a shiver down her spine.

'Cold?' Eric enquired solicitously. 'You could do with one of my whisky specials. Let me——'

'No, thanks.' Riona turned down the offer promptly. If a few glasses of champagne could make her light-headed, she didn't want to think what one of Eric's 'specials' would do. 'I need all my concentration to play,' she claimed, and it drew a sceptical look from the barman.

'The stuff you play——' his face reflected scorn '—is music to ride elevators to.'

Riona pulled a face back, but took no offence. 'I play what the customers want. You know that.'

'Aye, and I also know you're squandering your talent,' Eric declared with a sigh. 'Anyone who can play classical like you do shouldn't be wasting her time on sentimental slush for a bunch of philistines to get drunk to.'

'Music is music.' Riona shrugged, regretting having shown off to Eric the week before. The bar had been literally empty when she'd arrived and, with no one to object, she'd played a favourite Chopin piece. Not a particularly difficult piece, but it had left the barman impressed.

'Well, it's still a waste,' he stated with a clucking of his tongue, before going to serve a customer at the far end of the bar.

Riona took her chance to escape and went to sit down at the piano. She didn't need any music; she just had to hear a song a couple of times and she could play it.

By ten the bar had filled up. As usual, her audience was hardly what might be termed attentive. Couples tended to be absorbed in themselves and groups were often too noisy to notice the background music. It was only the occasional unattached male drinker who focused his attention on her, and then it was questionable if her playing was the attraction.

She had one tonight. She wasn't aware of him until one of the waiters appeared with a drink for her.

'You have an admirer,' the grinning waiter, Tommy, announced as she ended a number and he presented her with a fluted glass of some colourless liquid.

'What is it?' She sniffed at the sparkling drink.

'Champagne, of course!' Tommy tutted at her ignorance. 'That's what he asked for—the best champagne we serve. Do you want to know how much it costs a bottle?'

'Not particularly.' Riona pursed her lips.

'Well, do you want to know which one he is?' Tommy was clearly enjoying the situation.

'Not in the least,' she denied flatly.

Tommy still continued, 'He isn't your usual medallion man type. I mean, he's relatively sober, for a start. And, going on the champagne, he's not cheap. So, if you want my opinion——'

'I don't——' Riona put in futilely.

'I'd explore the possibilities,' Tommy advised with a wink, before taking himself off to serve other customers.

He left Riona muttering to herself as she placed the champagne, untouched, on the top of the piano. She felt no wish to explore any possibilities. She didn't even want to know who her admirer was.

She spent the rest of the evening counting down the minutes to twelve when she closed up shop. The bar itself didn't close until all the hotel residents had gone to bed, and that could be in the early hours.

It was still fairly busy when she did eventually finish. She passed a table of businessmen who were well on their way to being drunk, and one called out to her, but she kept walking. She guessed he might be the buyer of the champagne, and, having left it undrunk, she didn't feel she owed him any conversation.

All she wanted to do was get back to the boarding house and flop into bed. She collected her coat from Reception and, shrugging it on, walked down the entrance steps. It was dark now, but street-lights lit her path home along the river. It was a relatively short distance, and Riona didn't see the need for a taxi.

She didn't realise she was being followed until a voice called out, 'Hey, wait up, darling... and I'll walk you home.'

She turned to find one of the drunken businessmen a few paces behind her. He was a balding, paunchy forty-odd-year-old, with a sway in his step and an even sillier grin on his face. He looked harmless enough.

'It's all right,' Riona said, as he closed the gap. 'I haven't far to go.'

'Must walk you home,' he repeated, catching hold of her arm. 'Pretty girl like you shouldn't be walking alone. Lots of nasty characters about.'

Riona was beginning to realise that as he leered whisky fumes in her face. 'Really, I'd prefer to walk by myself.'

'Why...? Don't you trust me?' His tone switched from playfulness to belligerence rather easily. 'What do you think I'm going to do? Drag you down an alley or something?' he added with a laugh that rang a sour note.

'Of course not.' Riona told herself not to panic and tried to force a smile. 'I just don't want to put you to any bother.'

'It's no bother,' he echoed, and, giving her a look that made Riona wish she'd buttoned her coat, repeated, 'pretty girl like you... Which way?'

Riona pointed to the other side of the road, and found herself narrowly missing an oncoming car as he ushered them across. Then, as they started walking along the riverbank, away from the brighter lights, she began to get a little scared.

She stopped in front of a large house, and said, 'Well, thanks for walking me home.'

He didn't release her arm, saying instead, 'This is where you live?'

She nodded.

He looked up at the unlit house. 'Doesn't look like anybody's in.'

'I—er—my parents will be in bed,' she lied awkwardly.

He leered at her again. 'Then you can invite me in ... for a coffee.'

'I ... no ... I can't really. They might wake up.' She tried and failed to extricate her arm from his hold.

'Well, we can at least go round the back,' he went on. 'How about it?'

'What?' Riona couldn't believe he could be suggesting what she thought he was suggesting.

'You and me, darling,' he grunted, 'round the back.' And, before Riona had a chance to respond, he made a grab for her.

For a moment she was too shocked to react, as a clumsy hand grasped at her breast and squeezed, then the next moment he was pushing her hard against the garden gate and trying to kiss her. She lashed out wildly, with arms and legs, prepared to slap and kick until he let her go.

But Riona discovered, as many women had before her, that a man's drunken strength was far greater than a woman's. If he swore as her foot made contact with his shin, it only made him madder. He dragged her body against his and placed a sweaty palm over her mouth when she would have screamed.

'You like it rough, do you?' He actually smiled as he read the panic in her eyes, and, using his other hand, pulled up her dress.

Riona could do nothing. She stood there, gagging, wretching, screaming inside. She felt herself being lifted up, pushed through the gate, then all of a sudden falling free. She tried to scream, but, though her mouth was no longer covered, the sound dried up in her throat. She waited for his weight to slump on her, and instead saw him jerk backwards.

There was an arm locked round his throat, dragging him backwards, and it took Riona a moment to realise someone had come to her rescue. She stayed where she was, slumped against the garden gate, and heard, rather than saw, the crack of knuckles on bare flesh, the grunt of breath as a blow hit the stomach, then the echo of running feet on the pavement in retreat.

When a figure reappeared to kneel before her, she cringed, and a voice softly assured, 'It's me, Riona. You're OK. He's gone. You're OK. It's me.'

The voice was wonderfully familiar, and she raised her eyes in disbelief. But it was him, really him, and she gave a cry of relief as Cameron Adams's arms wrapped round her. She clung to him, crying, shaking, releasing all the fear that had kept her locked in silence during the attack.

He held her to him, saying nothing, until her tears had turned to dry sobs, then he gently lifted her from the step and drew her coat back round her now torn, dirty dress. He brushed the hair back from her face and asked, 'Can you walk?'

She nodded, and, ignoring the pain in one ankle, took a couple of limping steps back along the road. He stopped her there and made her sit on the garden wall while he examined her foot.

'I don't think it's broken,' he stated as he touched the already swelling ankle, 'but you've definitely sprained it... I'll have to carry you.'

Riona shook her head. 'It's all right. I'll try to walk.'

'You can't,' he told her simply, and, catching her chin in his hands, raised her face to his. 'You don't have to be scared of me. I won't hurt you. I'll never hurt you.'

His eyes made it a promise that reached the heart of her, and, in that moment, she gave him her trust—and, only half realising it, her love.

When he picked her up in his arms, she turned her head in his shoulder and once more wept. He carried her back along the way they'd come and Riona didn't question where they were going until they approached the hotel. Then she shook her head, and, pressing herself away from him, forced him to set her down.

'We can call a doctor from here,' he explained, 'and the police.'

Riona shook her head all the harder. 'No police,' she refused point-blank.

'You have to report him, Riona,' he insisted gently. 'You know what would have happened, if I hadn't followed you.'

Riona shuddered. She knew well enough. She just didn't want to relive it.

'You followed me?' she repeated, at last questioning how he came to be there.

'I decided to have dinner in town,' he relayed. 'Afterwards, I went for a drink in the cocktail bar, and who should I find as resident piano player? I assumed you weren't very pleased to be discovered when you didn't acknowledge my peace offering, so I——'

'Peace offering?'

'The champagne I sent over.'

'Oh, it was you. I thought...' Riona trailed off as she realised how she'd misunderstood.

'You thought it came from that guy,' Cameron concluded for her, and a hardness crept into his voice as he asked, 'Is that why you let him walk you home?'

Riona shook her head. 'I didn't let him. He just appeared.'

His brows collected in a frown. 'You didn't know him?'

Riona shook her head again.

'And you normally walk home on your own?' he added in disbelief.

This time Riona didn't answer, but her silence said it all.

'You are the craziest girl,' he sighed in exasperation. 'When I saw you walking off with the guy, I thought you must have agreed a meeting. I only followed because...well, never mind why. Just think what might have happened, if I hadn't,' he continued angrily.

Riona bowed her head. She had no defence. She'd acted stupidly.

Her misery was patent and his temper switched to her attacker. 'Still, you're safe now, and I'll make sure that bastard's going to be sorry he laid a finger on you. I reckon the police should find him pretty easily——'

'No, please,' Riona cut in, distressed, 'I don't want to go to the police. I don't want to go back to the hotel. I just want to go home.'

'To Invergair?' he guessed she meant, and, as the tears once more slipped down her face, he gave way. 'All right, I'll get you home. We can telephone the police tomorrow,' he murmured, and, lifting her in his arms again, walked round the hotel to the car park.

The car was warm and dark, and Riona sank back against the plush upholstery in exhaustion. He did not attempt any further conversation, and she was grateful. She just wanted to forget the whole incident. Though she'd done nothing wrong, she was the one left with a feeling of shame.

He drove quickly, and they arrived at her crofthouse in little more than an hour. She would have had him leave her at the front door, but he ignored her protests and carried her inside and upstairs.

He deposited her on the side of her bed, and she winced slightly as he jarred her ankle. 'I'll get the doctor.'

'Don't be silly!' she retorted with some of her usual spirit. 'It's two in the morning. You can't get the doctor out for a simple sprain.'

'I'm not sure it's that simple.' He knelt down to examine her swollen ankle.

She winced again. 'Well, your prodding it isn't doing much,' she muttered back, before realising how ungrateful it sounded.

He slanted her a dry look. 'You haven't lost any of your feistiness, at any rate.'

Feistiness? Riona wasn't sure what the word meant, but it didn't sound too complimentary, and she scowled a little.

He continued, impervious, 'Not that I particularly want you to. I'm kind of getting used to it... But a little common sense wouldn't go amiss, either.'

The last was said in a more serious vein, as he raised his eyes to her tear-stained face.

Riona understood what he meant, and, although she looked away, she admitted rather shamedly, 'I know. It was my fault. I should have taken a taxi instead of walking. I just didn't realise that sort of thing happened in Inverness.'

'It happens everywhere, Riona,' Cameron warned her. 'But it's *not* your fault. You're too innocent, that's all,' he said, brushing a strand of hair from her face.

It was a tender gesture, yet it wasn't tenderness Riona felt in return. Nor was it fear, although she drew back from him as if it were.

A pained frown creased his brow. 'You mustn't let this affect you, Riona. Right now, you feel revulsion at the touch of a man, and that's to be expected. But what happened tonight has nothing to do with sexual love, believe me,' he told her quietly. 'One day, when you meet a boy——'

'No!' Riona cut in, before he could say more. He didn't understand. 'I'm not... it's not how you think... Once I...' She tried to confess the truth to him.

'Hush. Don't talk any more.' He caught her hand and squeezed it. 'You need to rest. I'll go get a cold compress for your ankle, while you change for bed. All right?'

She nodded, too tired to argue. He went out of the room, and she slipped off her coat and the now soiled dress, and put on the old shirt she usually slept in. It had been one of her grandfather's, handed down to her when she'd grown out of her childhood nightgowns. Being the sort with long tails and a high collar, it covered her respectably.

Cameron Adams eventually reappeared, carrying a couple of wet cloths. 'You don't have a refrigerator,' he commented with some disbelief, 'so I couldn't make up an ice pack.'

'We've never needed one.' She shrugged, then winced a little as he wrapped a cloth round her ankle. In a moment or two, however, some of the throbbing heat went out of the swelling.

He switched cloths when the first lost its cooling effect, and went through to the bathroom to re-soak it in cold water. He acted with the impersonality of a doctor, and Riona soon got over any embarrassment. He repeated this routine several times until he noticed she was actually nodding off to sleep on him, then he pulled back the bedclothes and helped her into bed, tucking the sheets round her.

Riona felt no fear at his presence, just a gratitude for what he had done for her. She was too tired to express it, but she smiled at him in acceptance as he sat on the chair by the bed and watched over her until she drifted off to sleep.

She woke in the night, screaming. What she'd refused to relive awake had come back in dreams. Only this time there was no one to save her; this time she had to suffer the stench of the man's sweating body, the vileness of his breath, the weight of him crushing her to the ground.

She screamed and screamed, but no one came and he held on to her, and she struck out with her hands until he shouted back at her, 'Riona, wake up! Riona, it's me. You're all right. You're all right. Wake up.'

His hands framed her face, forcing her head up, forcing her to look at him, to see not her attacker but her saviour, and her screams died away. She went still for a moment, then sobbed in relief as his arms came round her to keep her safe.

He held her to him as he would a child, stroking her hair, crooning to her, 'Hush, hush. It's just a dream. Only a dream. Go back to sleep.'

Freed from her nightmare, in time Riona did just that. She fell asleep in his arms. She fell asleep, feeling warm and safe and loved.

At dawn she woke with the same feeling. As the first rays of sun filtered through the thin curtains, she woke to find his body next to hers, her arm across his bare chest, her head turned into his shoulder. He was naked except for undershorts, but she felt no panic. In that first moment it seemed as natural as breathing to be lying with him like that. Only when her mind took over, whispering immoralities and impossibilities, did she try to draw away.

He did not wake, but his arms automatically drew her back, a hand slipping down to her hips, curving her body to his. The breath caught in Riona's throat. She still wore her nightshirt, but she felt the heat of him through it. She moaned a little in protest, but it was the softest of sounds, and became part of his dreams, as he groaned in response, and, rolling over, pressed her back against the mattress.

'Cameron.' She said his name in breathless appeal, the second before his mouth came down on hers.

With his body covering hers, trapping her against the bed, Riona might have believed herself back in the nightmare of her attack, yet she didn't. She didn't even think of it. For this was a world away from last night, with no brutality in his kiss, no wish to hurt or humiliate in the hands that caressed her.

He kissed her softly at first, passion still dormant, and for a moment Riona lay there, passive. Then his lips began to move on hers, seeking, tasting, needing more, until she felt desire begin to flow like a river through her veins. Her lips parted for him, and he made some sound of satisfaction before thrusting into the warm, sweet recesses of her mouth with an intimacy that shocked her senses.

Whether it was pain or pleasure he offered, Riona wasn't sure, but she seemed incapable of resistance. When he finally took his mouth from hers, breathing hard, he whispered her name, and she knew he was no longer dreaming. She did not ask for release. When he rolled back on his side and caught her eyes with his, she simply stared back at him in acceptance.

He reached out a hand to cup her cheek, and, frowning a little, said, 'I think I may be in love with you, Riona Macleod.'

The admission was a reluctant one and Riona neither believed nor disbelieved. It didn't seem to matter. For she was certain of one thing. Against the odds, against all sense and reason, *she* loved *him*. And that was what kept her there, lying beside him, waiting, wanting.

Her face reflected her feelings, as his hand slowly trailed downwards to trace the curve of her neck and shoulder, before stopping at her nightshirt. He unbuttoned the front without hurry. He barely touched her, giving her all the time in the world to protest, to pull away. He made it clear he would never force her. If she was caught, it was by her own compulsion.

She quivered a little as the sides of the shirt parted, but she did not try to hide herself. His hand fell away, and it was his eyes that touched the bareness of her flesh and grew opaque with desire at the sight of her breasts, soft and full, rose-tipped, wholly feminine as they pushed out from the masculine shirt. Then he lifted his hand again, to draw away the shirt, easing it down one arm until her upper body was almost naked. Once more he stared at her, needing no words to tell her he found her beautiful, and Riona realised, as his eyes lost focus, that he was already making love to her in his mind. It scared her, the way he looked at her, the strength of his desire coming in waves, yet she lay there, unmoving, powerless, wanting to be dragged under.

He reached for her, unbearably slow, unbelievably gentle, his hand following the curve of her waist, seeking softer, fuller flesh. When he touched her breast, it was the lightest of caresses, his fingers barely brushing against her skin before spreading upwards to her collar-bone, but it sent a spasm of desire through her. She longed for—and feared—his next move, and felt almost cheated when, instead of touching her breast again, he ran his hand down her arm, from shoulder to thigh. She didn't realise his intention until his head bent towards her.

She cried out. She couldn't help it. He took her breast in his mouth, and circled the hard peak of it with his tongue, and sent her senses reeling so far that she cried out.

Her response was all Cameron might have wanted and more, as he pushed her back down on the bed, and, stripping off her nightshirt, began to satisfy his own needs. Rough and sensual, he played and bit and sucked at her yielding flesh with his mouth, pleasuring her until the soft, sweet moans of her desire threatened his own control.

When he lifted his head away, it was to look down at her, hair already matted with sweat, lips parted, her eyes wide and staring. The girl had become a woman so desirable he could have taken her then and there and not worried about the consequences. But still her vulnerability caught at him, reminded him of the fifteen years and the whole different world that lay between them.

'Riona.' He threaded his hand through her hair and forced her to look at him. 'I need to hear you say it. Say you want me.'

'Want you?' She echoed the words without meaning.

'Or tell me to stop,' he said, his voice harshening. 'Only do it now, not later!'

'I . . .' Riona shook her head, confused by the change in him.

She didn't understand what he was really asking, didn't understand it was her inexperience that made him curse, 'Goddammit,' even as he pushed her back down on the bed and fastened his mouth to hers.

He kissed her as if he wanted to punish her for something, and Riona moaned in protest. But, when he made to draw away, to leave her, she clung to him, and without words, told him how much she wanted him. He gave a groan of satisfaction as his mouth left hers to trail across her cheek, biting gently on her ear, moving downwards to the softness of her throat, seeking to excite once more in slow, tormenting ways.

As his lips touched the pulse at the base of her throat, her body curved to his in instinctive invitation, and his hand went to her hips, holding her to him. She felt the hardness of his body, and her own arousal became tinged with fear. But it was too late to stop now, far too late, for, while his lips began a slow journey down the valley between her breasts, his hand was slipping inside the briefs she still wore, pushing them down over her hips, over her thighs, until she was naked. And all the time he kept kissing her with that clever, knowing mouth, licking at the fine sheen of perspiration on her soft skin, reaching down as far as the flat of her stomach, then up again to briefly suck her swollen nipples and make her cry out with wanting once more.

He left her for a moment and Riona opened her eyes to see him standing by the bed, looking down at her. In that instant she felt no shame. She felt just love and desire, incalculable and inseparable. She watched as he removed his shorts and still felt no embarrassment, only wonder at the powerful beauty of his body. When he lay down beside her again, she placed her hand on his muscled chest, tanned many shades darker than her own skin and covered with fine hair, damp with sweat. She followed the line of it down to his navel, then spread her hand across his flat abdomen as far as the coarser hair below. But she was too shy to touch him and he sensed it, as he laughed a little before lifting her hand to his mouth and kissing its palm.

'This time's for you,' he growled softly, as he rolled her back over on the bed to kiss her with gentle passion on the mouth.

And it was for her, that first time. He treated her like a virgin. He kissed her until she breathed his name. He held her to him until any fear was dispelled. He touched her body until every part of her knew him and wanted him—and only then, when she was ready, did he take what she so willingly offered.

He treated her like a virgin, only she wasn't. As he poised above her, his face blurred into another, younger, leaner face. She thought of Fergus—her first lover—and, at the very moment Cameron entered her, her eyes shut in pain at the memory.

He saw and misunderstood, and gathered her into his arms. 'Oh, God, I hurt you. I tried not to. I shouldn't have——'

'No. No.' Riona shook her head and before he could say more, say words she didn't deserve, she found his mouth with hers. She kissed him hard, urging him to go on, to make her forget there ever had been another man, and, as her fingers bit painfully into his shoulder, he pushed inside her once more.

He thrust hard and Riona whimpered in shock at the pleasure it brought. She arched towards him, and he thrust again, pushing higher, filling her, drawing back as she moaned for him, lifting her to him, thrusting. Over and over their bodies moved in the rhythm of love, beautiful bodies glistening with sweat, perfect love offering all, prolonging pleasure until it was a sweet agony they could bear no longer.

For Riona, it was like drowning, losing herself inside him, losing who she was, who he was, even as they came together and she called out his name and he spilled his seed in her. It was like dying, a complete release, floating bodiless, careless, leaving behind all the realities that made being with him an insanity.

She stayed in that state for three impossibly wonderful weeks. He told her he loved her time after time and she believed him. He wanted to take over her life and she let him. He had her give up her work in Inverness, dismissing her need for the money, and begged her to return to America with him, until, caught up in the dream, she agreed. But, worst of all, he made love to her continually, everywhere and anywhere, made her need him like a drug, made her so obsessed that she could have died of sorrow when he left.

He gave her no warning. One morning he went to Glasgow to see the estate solicitors and failed to return. She waited a couple of days, fearing an accident, then heard in the village store that the laird had flown back to America. She waited another two weeks, hoping every day would bring a letter, before she finally accepted the truth.

He'd gone and he wasn't coming back.

CHAPTER FIVE

RIONA'S mind returned to the present and the baby now asleep in her arms. She carried him upstairs to the cot beside her bed and tucked him under the quilt, then sat watching over him for a while. He was so perfect, so beautiful; it was hard to believe he'd come out of such pain.

Two months had passed before she discovered she was pregnant. She'd been too miserable to eat so she'd actually lost weight. She'd also driven herself hard, trying to ignore the needs of her body, ignoring the changes. She'd worked from dawn to dusk on the croft, pushing herself until she was too tired to dream, punishing herself for being stupid.

Then one day the doctor had turned up at the croft, taken one look at her wretched appearance and insisted on examining her. She supposed she'd known deep down.

At any rate, she felt little surprise when he announced, 'Well, lass, you're pregnant. Coming up to three months, I'd say.'

She felt no joy, either, accepting his diagnosis in silence. She had no one to blame but herself.

'I assume it's Cameron's,' the doctor added wearily, and that *had* surprised her.

Neither she nor Cameron had advertised their brief affair. Much of the time they'd spent round the croft, in and out of bed. They'd gone to Edinburgh for a few days, but had seen more of their hotel room than Scotland's capital. She'd refused him only one thing, and that was to stay overnight in Invergair Hall, for there he was the laird and she his tenant. They'd kept their relationship a secret rather than have it the subject of gossip.

'Why should you think it was Cameron Adams's?' She hoped the doctor was guessing in the dark.

He wasn't. 'I came up one day to check on that sprained ankle you had. You weren't in the house, but the collie found you for me...up in the heather, you and Cameron. I didn't see you, but I heard you laughing and came away.'

Riona's face reddened. He obviously knew they'd been more than laughing.

'Don't worry,' the doctor added, 'I've no told anybody, and, as far as I know, there's been no talk about the two of you... Is he coming back?'

She shook her head. She couldn't say for certain. He'd put in a factor to manage the estate and there was talk of a woman coming down from Edinburgh to help organise a knitting co-operative. He could be back tomorrow or he might never be back. The only thing she knew for sure was he wouldn't be coming back to her.

'Right, well, you'll have to write to him about this.' He nodded towards her still flat stomach.

She shook her head again. 'I can't,' she said simply.

The doctor misunderstood, declaring, 'Then I'll do it for you, lass.'

'No, I don't want him to know. It's my problem, not his.'

'Rubbish! It takes two to make a baby, and it's his responsibility. What's more, if Cameron's half the man I think he is, he'll be back on the first plane to marry you.'

Riona's eyes closed at the suggestion. The doctor might be a lovely old man, but he really hadn't a clue. The time had passed when couples married because they had to, and she wouldn't have wanted such a solution had it been on offer.

Cameron had made it clear from the start of their affair that he wasn't ready for fatherhood. He'd dressed it up a little, saying she was too young to be a mother, that she'd barely begun her own life, that he wanted her all to himself for a while. At the time it had seemed his concern was mostly for her, but, when he'd walked out on her, Riona had realised the truth. It was Cameron who wanted no ties and had done his best to avoid them. No matter how spontaneously they had made love, he'd still taken care that there would be no consequences. Even that first time he'd driven her down the next day to the doctor's surgery so she might ask for something called 'a morning-after pill'.

Only what had sounded commonplace and common sense to a man of the world like Cameron had been a matter of acute embarrassment when faced with Dr Macnab. She'd hoped to get his younger partner, and instead found herself sitting across the desk from a man who had treated her like a favourite niece for as long as she could remember. She'd left the surgery with her sprained ankle professionally bandaged and that was all. She'd let Cameron believe otherwise and had allowed herself to become pregnant. In her eyes that made the baby her problem.

She hadn't changed her mind, although the doctor had tried to make her do so throughout her pregnancy. Any time she was tempted to weaken, she'd recall Cameron's words, 'Babies should be planned and wanted; otherwise they're a disaster.' Those words had effectively killed dead any idea of contacting him. For this wasn't a wanted baby—not by Cameron, at any rate, when he'd been so careful to avoid its conception.

She still felt the same, even now, when Cameron had returned. The baby was hers and hers alone. He might be the image of his father but the local gossips didn't know it, for she'd kept Rory away from curious eyes. Only Dr Macnab and Mrs Ross could betray her, and they wouldn't. She just had to keep Rory out of Cameron's way, and that should be simple enough if she stayed on the croft. She couldn't believe he'd actually come looking for her.

* * *

She was wrong. She hadn't been able to predict Cameron's actions then, and she couldn't now. He came, not that night but the next. It was almost ten. She heard the sound of hammering on her door and knew instantly who was there.

She went through to the hall to check the lock was on. He must have heard her approach, for he called out, 'Open the door, Riona!'

She made no move to do so. She didn't want him in her house. It would evoke too many memories.

'Open it up or I'll bust it down!' he threatened at her lack of response.

He sounded angry but in control. She remained silent, not believing he'd carry out the threat.

She was mistaken. He repeated, 'Open up, Riona,' in the same low, urgent tone, gave her about thirty seconds to answer, then responded accordingly.

It was a foot he used, kicking hard against the lock. The first kick had little effect, as did the second, but the third splintered the surrounding wood.

'All right.' She realised another kick might take the door off its hinges. 'I'll open it. Just give me a minute.'

Her appeal worked. The attack on the door ceased. She ran upstairs to check on Rory.

He was sleeping, despite the noise outside. She closed the door of his room and raced back downstairs to the living-room. There was one picture of him on the mantelpiece. She shoved it in a drawer.

'*Riona*?' Cameron's voice came to her again, rising in temper.

She hurried to the door and finally opened it. He didn't wait for an invitation but brushed past her into the house.

'Where is he?' His eyes ranged up the narrow staircase to her bedroom.

'Who?' she asked, although the answer was obvious enough.

'The baby,' he rapped back, and would have gone up the stairs if she hadn't grabbed his arm.

Her grip was strong and desperate, but he could still have shaken her loose, had he chosen to. Instead he turned to take hold of her by the arms, dragging her close enough to see the fury in his eyes.

'He's mine, isn't he?' he growled at her. 'The baby's mine...'

'No.' She shook her head. 'No, he's not. I told you——'

'You lying bitch,' he cut across her. 'I know what you told me, but that's not what Macnab says.'

'The doctor?' Riona was shocked. Surely he hadn't betrayed her? He couldn't have. 'You're the one who's lying. The doctor wouldn't tell you anything.'

'Not outright, no,' he rasped back, 'but when I asked if you were getting support from Fergus Ross, he was stunned by the idea. Clearly he doesn't believe responsibility lies in that quarter, so that leaves me.'

'There might have been someone else,' Riona claimed wildly, then wished she hadn't.

He came back with a brutal, 'There might have been several, for all I know. You were certainly eager enough for it.'

'Why, you...' She tried to free a hand to slap his face.

But he tightened his grip and forced her back against the wall. 'Come on, honey, let's not go through the shocked virgin routine again. I've never met a woman with better moves. You had me wanting you every minute of the day.'

Riona's face flamed as she remembered. The wanting had been mutual. They had been consumed with each other. What had gone wrong?

She looked up at him, her eyes a reflection of the hurt and bewilderment she'd felt at his sudden departure. Why had he left? Had it just been sex for him? Was it *her* love that had scared him off?

'Don't bother!' He pushed her body away from his. 'I don't get taken for a sucker twice. The baby—that's all I'm interested in. You want to guess what the doctor said when I asked if I was the father?'

Riona shook her head. 'He didn't tell you. I know he didn't,' she insisted, giving herself away with every word.

'Oh, he didn't tell me,' he echoed in agreement. 'The old man said nothing—absolutely nothing. Which is exactly my point.'

Riona frowned. She didn't see it.

'Macnab might still be fooled by your Little Miss Innocent act,' he continued harshly, 'but he wouldn't lie for you. And it's pretty obvious he *believes* I'm the father.'

'So?' Riona tried to bluff it out. 'That doesn't *make* you the father. Maybe I lied to him.'

'Maybe.' His lips formed a sneer. 'You're capable of it, at any rate.'

'That's rich,' she threw back, 'coming from you.'

'Oh, yeah? When did I ever lie to you?' he had the nerve to counter.

Riona stared at him in disbelief. Had he forgotten that once he had told her he loved her? Had he forgotten running out on her just days later?

She remembered. The hurt might have left her, but the bitterness remained.

'What are you doing here?' she demanded, her eyes growing as hard as glass. 'You can't want the baby to be yours, so why don't you just take my word for it and go?'

He shook his head. 'You're dead right. I don't want it to be mine. I don't want a part of you in a part of me. But, if it is mine, do you think I'm going to leave its upbringing to you?' He looked at her with contempt, then looked around at the poverty of her surroundings. 'So, where is he? In your bedroom?'

He made to go upstairs again and she clutched hold of his sleeve. 'You can't go up there. He's asleep!' she cried at him.

'Somehow I doubt that, the racket you're making,' he ground back, and, throwing off her hand, took the stairs in a few strides.

Riona followed, but was helpless to stop him. He found her bedroom easily. He should do. They had lain together there often enough.

He entered the room and crossed to the cot, visible in the glow from a night-light. She stayed at the door. She prayed that Rory would still be asleep. If he was, Cameron would only see the back of his dark head.

Her prayers weren't answered. A gurgling noise came from the cot. Rory rarely cried when he woke. Even with a stranger standing over his cot, he did not cry. He already had his father's confidence in life.

He also had his father's hair and eyes and mouth. She was sure Cameron would see that. She assumed he did, when he leaned into the cot and picked the child out of it. He held his son at arm's length and stared hard at him for a moment, then carried him to where Riona stood.

His eyes shifted to her, with a look of intense dislike, and she reeled a little as he thrust the baby into her arms. She waited for the accusations and recriminations, but none came. Instead he pushed past her and retook the stairs. She didn't fully realise his intention until she heard the front door bang loudly behind her.

He had gone. He had done what he'd come to do and left. He had failed to see it. He'd looked at his son without recognition, and once more walked out of her life.

The baby began to cry now, although he could not have understood what had just happened. Riona cradled him close. 'Never mind, baby, you have me, you have me,' she crooned over and over, even as the tears slipped down her face.

For all her words and her actions, till then she'd held on to a small part of the dream. She'd sat some nights and imagined Cameron coming back, sorry he'd left, realising he loved her, loving her more when he discovered she'd had his son. That was what happened in novels and stories.

But this was real life. In real life he came back for business reasons—she'd heard he was selling the estate—and, discovering she'd had a child, acted out of moral obligation. All the time he'd been hoping the child wasn't his; small wonder that he'd seen no likeness, felt no bond. Just like the last time, he'd walked away without a backward glance.

That was what Riona thought, but once again she was proved wrong when she met him a couple of days later. It was on the Sunday. Though she'd stopped playing at the ceilidh and at church since her pregnancy, she still went to the doctor's for lunch. The day was pleasantly warm and she walked the three miles to the village with Rory in an old pram. He was sound asleep by the time she arrived and she parked the pram at the front door.

The doctor must have been looking out for her as he opened the door without her knocking, and she said, 'Rory's asleep, so I think I'll leave him outside for a while.

'Aye, the fresh air'll do him good,' Dr Macnab agreed, as he let her into the house. She was well inside the hall before he added, 'I have a visitor, lass.'

'Visitor?' She didn't catch on, until a second figure appeared in the sitting-room doorway.

Their eyes met and held for a moment. He didn't look surprised. Obviously he'd known she was coming.

She tried to back out of the door and the doctor stopped her.

'Now, lass, I know how you feel, but you can't just run away,' he told her sternly. 'Pride's one thing, but you have to consider the baby. If Cameron's prepared to help the two of you——'

'Why should he?' Riona asked the question of the doctor, but her eyes winged back to Cameron. He looked coolly indifferent. 'I've told him the baby isn't his. That's all he needs to know.'

'Lass, lass.' The doctor shook his head at her. 'You can't go on like this. You have to accept that——'

'The baby's mine,' Cameron interrupted tersely. 'I know it. You know it. And a test will prove it. So let's just cut the crap.'

She winced a little at his words, while the doctor said more gently, 'He's right, Riona. There's no point. Fatherhood can now be conclusively established.'

'That's apart from the obvious fact the boy's mine,' Cameron added, without the slightest trace of warmth in his voice or his eyes.

Riona stared back at him, unable to believe she'd once loved this man. Had she been blind to the coldness in him, the cruelty?

'Look,' the doctor appealed, 'why don't we all go into the dining-room and discuss the matter over lunch? I'm sure we can come to some sort of arrangement...'

Riona shook her head. She wasn't going to sit down to Sunday lunch with Cameron Adams. She wasn't going to come to any arrangement.

'I want nothing from you.' Her tone was one of contempt.

'What you want is of no interest to me,' he returned coldly. 'It's the child's needs that concern me.'

'And you don't think they concern me?' She went on the defensive.

'I never said that.' He was cool and collected in the face of her rising temper, but that hardly made Riona feel better. 'I'm sure you look after him adequately on a day-to-day level, but have you considered the future— *his* future?'

'Of course I have,' she claimed angrily.

'And?' A questioning brow was lifted in her direction.

Riona opened her mouth, then shut it again, finding no suitable response. She knew too well what he was getting at. He didn't have to spell it out.

He did anyway, saying, 'Correct me if I'm wrong. You have no money. Nor is there any prospect of your having any. Which can only mean you're planning to bring up my son on the pittance you make from the croft and possibly some welfare hand-outs.'

'Cameron, man,' the doctor urged him to go easier, as Riona visibly flinched.

But he ignored the older man, rasping a final, 'Well?' at her.

'I—I...' Riona felt helpless, with no weapons to fight back. He had summed up her life with dreadful precision. 'I have other plans,' she finally claimed. 'I may move to Edinburgh.'

'And do what?' he pursued at this vague suggestion. 'Live in some low-rent apartment? Farm out Rory while you work? And work at what?'

'I—I...' Riona had asked all these questions of herself a thousand times. She didn't need him to point out how limited her opportunities were. 'That's my business,' she said at last, recovering a little of her spirit.

'Uh-huh!' He shook his head. 'Not since you went ahead and had my child it isn't.'

Riona's eyes narrowed at his choice of words. 'Presumably you wouldn't have had me "go ahead" with the pregnancy, if you'd known,' she concluded bluntly.

'Riona,' the doctor interceded again, 'I'm sure Cameron didn't mean it like that.'

'Didn't he?' It was Riona's turn to direct the American an accusing look.

He returned it, grating, 'If that's your justification for not telling me, then you can shove it. I had the right to know, at least.'

'What did you expect,' Riona flared back, 'a little note informing you of the impending event? Well, yes, I suppose I could have sent one—had I known your address. But then you left in such a hurry, didn't you?'

A look of fury constricted his handsome features. 'Whose fault was that?'

'I...' Riona's mouth dropped open at the nerve of him trying to shift the blame.

He continued relentlessly, 'And don't give me that bull about not knowing my address. Anything sent to Invergair Hall would have been forwarded.'

'So?' Riona couldn't believe he was making her out to be the villain of the piece. 'What was I supposed to write? "Dear Cameron, Remember me, the Scottish girl you had a brief fling with? Well, I just thought you'd like to know I'm having your baby. Best wishes, Riona." Would that have pleased your lairdship?' she said in scathing tones.

'Possibly not,' he admitted in a voice of ice, 'but that's irrelevant. As the child's father, I still have rights and responsibilities.'

Riona frowned back. She hadn't imagined he had any rights. Surely he was bluffing? She shot a glance of enquiry at Dr Hamish, but the old man raised his shoulders, unaware of the legal position either.

'You have no rights,' she declared uncertainly, and it drew a cold, superior smile.

'You think not. I could fight you for custody,' Cameron ran inexorably on, 'and there's an outside chance I might win. At the very least an American court would award me visitation rights... However, I don't think a messy court battle would be in Rory's interests, do you?'

He waited for an answer, but Riona had none. She sensed there was worse to come than threats of court action.

'Come, now, man, you and Riona can surely work things out without involving the lawyers,' Dr Hamish spoke up, still hoping to put matters on a friendlier footing. 'The only people who would benefit out of that would be the lawyers themselves.'

'Exactly.' Cameron took it as support for his argument.

'Well, in that case——' The doctor began to say something, but Riona cut across him.

'What do you want?' She was tired of this fencing; it was time to hear the bottom line.

'Several things,' he clipped back. 'First, I want the boy to have my name.'

'Your name?' Riona repeated blankly.

'Yes.'

'But...you expect me to re-register him as Adams?'

Riona's tone told him how ridiculous she found the idea. It turned out, however, to be slightly less ridiculous than what he really meant.

'Hardly.' An impatient look accused her of deliberate stupidity. 'When I say I want him to have my name, I mean I wish him to have legitimate status.'

'Legitimate status?' Riona echoed him once more as she tried to catch up with where the conversation was going.

Dr Hamish was quicker, a smile appearing on his craggy face as he said, 'Ah, Cameron, man, I told her you'd do the right thing by her. I just wish she'd written you earlier. Never mind, all's well that ends well.'

'What?' Riona didn't yet feel she understood.

A patently delighted doctor helped her out, saying, 'He wants to marry you, lass. He wants to marry you.'

She switched incredulous eyes to Cameron, seeking a denial. Instead, in cold, unemotional tones, he confirmed, 'I'm prepared to marry you, yes. I believe, under Scottish law, that doing so will automatically legitimise Rory, despite the lapse between birth and marriage.'

'Yes, that's so.' An enthusiastic doctor nodded, while Riona continued to stare at Cameron, wondering if he actually *believed* she'd be prepared to marry him. Could he be so arrogant? Did he imagine she'd be grateful?

'Well?' he demanded an answer.

'I won't marry you.' She didn't hide her disgust at the idea. 'I wouldn't marry you even if you went down on bended knee and begged me.'

'Riona!' The doctor despaired at this abrasive response.

Cameron Adams was less disconcerted, bluntly informing her, 'I'm talking of a marriage of convenience for the purposes of legitimising our son. I won't want to consummate it.' His expression betrayed an antipathy that matched her own.

'Och, the two of you!' The doctor was impatient with what he saw as foolish pride. 'You were once fond enough of each other to make a baby; you could be fond again. If you'd only discuss what went wrong, try to——'

'Doctor!' The last thing Riona wanted was a post-mortem on their relationship. Cameron had walked out on her when he'd got bored. What more was there to say?

Cameron seemed to share her opinion, as, in clipped tones, he continued, 'This is what I propose. We marry in Scotland by special licence and return to the States. You stay there for a time—six months, say—to give the appearance of a conventional marriage, then return here claiming incompatibility. I shall fly over periodically to visit Rory, until he's old enough to spend his vacations with me in the States.'

'And why should I agree to all this?' Riona assumed he was going to offer some inducement to her.

She was right, as he ran on, 'If you do, I'll guarantee you lifetime's use of Invergair Hall, an appropriate sum to run it and an allowance for both you and Rory. That way he will grow up with an appreciation of his inheritance.'

'His what?' He was moving too fast again for Riona.

'I have abandoned plans to sell Invergair. Instead I have decided to cede it to Rory on his twenty-fifth birthday.'

'The Hall?'

'And the estate.'

Riona had to stop her mouth from dropping open. He was calmly talking about giving away what was rumoured to be six million pounds' worth of property to a baby he'd barely seen. She realised once again that she had never really known or understood Cameron.

'You're going to hand Invergair over to Rory?' She wanted to be sure she'd got it right.

He nodded, then qualified, 'Unless he proves himself unfit to run it.'

Riona frowned at what sounded like a catch. 'In what way unfit?'

'If he had a drug addiction, an alcohol problem or was simply incompetent,' he reeled off possibilities. 'I certainly wouldn't turn over Invergair to someone who was likely to squander it.'

Riona conceded his point, but still found the conversation unreal. Here they were, facing each other in the doctor's hallway, discussing twenty-five years into the future. She tried to imagine herself mistress of the Hall and failed.

'There are certain other conditions attached,' he added, with the same deadly calm.

'Such as?' Riona knew already she wouldn't like them.

'Should you remarry or wish to cohabit with someone before Rory was eighteen, possession of the Hall and custody of Rory would revert to me,' he stated. 'You would, of course, get visitation rights.'

'That's monstrous!' Riona protested angrily, although she had no thoughts of remarriage—or even marriage, period. 'Why are you trying to punish me, Cameron? What have I ever done to you?'

A flicker of something—it looked like pain—crossed his face, but was quickly gone. 'You don't come into it.' His voice reflected indifference. 'I'm simply ensuring Rory doesn't have some stepfather or so-called "uncle" thrust on him at some vulnerable stage of his life.'

'Now, Cameron, you're being unfair,' the doctor stepped in, as the atmosphere turned sour once more.

'You're not offering Riona a proper marriage, and at the same time you're condemning her to a life of loneliness.'

Cameron's lips thinned at the doctor's analysis. 'I'm safeguarding my son's interests and his future position as laird. If she feels the need for a man, she can always go away for a dir—discreet weekend to Edinburgh.' He changed mid-sentence but it was obvious what word he was going to use. The curl of his lip told her that.

Riona paled as she thought of their own few days in Edinburgh. Had that just been a dirty weekend to him, too?

'Now, just a minute, Cameron.' Dr Macnab came to her defence. 'I've known the lass here all her life, and, though she might have gone with you, she's not the type to sleep around.'

'Isn't she?' Cameron stared past the doctor to Riona. 'That's what I thought, Doc, but I wised up. I suggest you do the same. Why don't you ask her about Fergus Ross? Ask her how often she'd been with him.'

'No, no.' The doctor shook his head. 'You've quite the wrong idea. Fergus and Riona have been friends since childhood, but that's all. If someone told you otherwise——'

'Oh, someone did,' Cameron cut in, 'only I was too stupid to listen. Isobel Fraser told me Fergus Ross had practically lived up at your croft on his last leave,' he directed at Riona, 'but I chose to believe it was all innocent boy-girl stuff. After all, you were still a virgin when we met, weren't you?' A sneer made his face almost ugly.

'I never told you that,' Riona claimed in her own defence.

It drew a bitter laugh. 'No, you just let me think it and go right ahead and make a fool of myself.'

Dr Macnab looked from one angry face to another, and, still believing it was a simple matter of misunderstanding, appealed, 'Calm down, both of you. I don't know who's said what to whom, but I certainly wouldn't go by Isobel Fraser's word. If you didn't know it, Isobel had her eye on you herself, Cameron, lad. That's why she up and left after you yourself went.'

'Maybe,' Cameron conceded, holding Riona's gaze, 'but she was still telling the truth in this case. She didn't even know about us. I mentioned the fact that you were struggling to keep the croft going and that I needed one of the estate workers to help with repairs. She suggested that your difficulties might be temporary as Fergus Ross would be home soon on leave and would probably move in with you again. I didn't believe her. I was so sure of you, I thought, if Fergus does return, you'll choose me. How wrong can a man be?' He scoffed at his own naïveté.

Riona shook her head, betraying herself as she replied softly, 'But I would have. You know I would——'

'Like hell!' he exploded back at her. 'You chose Fergus. We both know that... And why not? After all, he was your first lover, wasn't he? And before you deny it, that didn't come from Isobel, but the man himself.'

Riona stared at him blankly, while the doctor concluded, 'Fergus told you this.'

Cameron nodded. 'Only he didn't just tell me, he boasted of having the prettiest girl in Invergair—with the emphasis on "having"... I assume he informed you of our accidental meeting,' he threw at Riona.

She continued to stare at him until suddenly the truth hit her hard.

Fergus had been at sea when Cameron had appeared on the scene. She hadn't been expecting him back when he'd suddenly turned up on a weekend pass. It had been the night Cameron had been away in Glasgow and she remembered being relieved at his absence, as Fergus had arrived on her doorstep late. He'd hitched home and it had been dark when a tourist had picked him up and delivered him to the foot of her road. An American tourist, Riona recalled Fergus's words at the time, but only now understood their significance. How stupid she'd been not to see the connection then!

Cameron saw realisation dawn on her face, and he twisted the knife. 'You see, I changed my mind about staying overnight. I drove back from Glasgow and picked up this kid on the road. He was anxious to get home to his girlfriend and I gave him a ride to the bottom of her hill. It was late at night, but he was sure of his welcome. I waited two, three hours, but it seems he was right. I drove past the next morning and saw him on the road. The sun was just up. I kept driving.'

He spoke with a hard, factual edge, as if he no longer cared. His pride had been hurt, but that was all.

For Riona, only now learning the truth, it was as if it had just happened. She imagined Fergus, full of himself, having to show off, confiding to a stranger what should have been private. Perhaps he had mentioned her name then been encouraged to say more. And Cameron, she imagined him sitting at the bottom of her road, giving her a chance, waiting for a couple of hours, waiting for her to turn Fergus away. Only she hadn't and it had spoiled everything.

'Didn't he want you,' Cameron added cruelly, 'when the baby turned out to be mine?'

'I...' Riona couldn't speak; she was hurting too much.

He was merciless, continuing, 'Maybe he wasn't such a mug as me. Maybe he didn't fancy a lifetime of wondering who you were going to cheat with next.'

Riona shook her head, appealing for him to understand. It wasn't the way he thought. The fault might be hers, for not telling him about Fergus, but it hadn't been like that.

'That's enough!' was directed at him by an angry Dr Macnab. 'Can't you see what you're doing to her?'

Cameron's eyes remained on Riona. He saw all right. He wanted her hurt. Her tears didn't move him.

'I think you'd better go,' Dr Macnab told him, and, not waiting for a response, turned to gather Riona in his arms. 'Hush, lass, hush. I know, I know. It isn't true. Hush, lass . . .'

His words made her cry all the harder, while Cameron, making a sound of disgust, pushed past them, out of the door. He slammed it hard behind him.

With the door shut, it was a moment or two before Riona heard Rory crying. When she did, she put her own misery second, and, freeing herself from the doctor's comforting arms, hurried outside.

She was too late. Cameron had picked up Rory from his pram and was holding him on high. Rory had ceased crying and was staring round-eyed down at the man. Riona's heart froze.

Her fear must have been written all over her face as Cameron turned and, lowering the baby to his shoulder, said, 'You think I'd do that? Just take the baby?'

Riona remained silent, for that was exactly what she'd thought on seeing Rory in his arms.

'Here.' He handed the baby back to her. 'I don't intend to kidnap him. You've heard my proposition. I'll wait your answer.'

'You can have it now,' she said, feeling stronger with Rory in her arms. 'I won't marry you, not in any circumstances.'

'Fair enough.' He accepted rejection rather easily, but then added, 'I'll see you in court.'

'Court?' Riona echoed in fright, remembering his threat of a custody battle.

'You don't think I'm going to give up my son so easily?' he went on relentlessly. 'I suggest you find yourself a good lawyer. I already have.'

'Lawyer?' Riona echoed again, shaking her head. 'But I don't know any lawyers. And I have no money . . .'

'That's your problem,' he dismissed coldly, and, before she could appeal for reason, turned on his heel and walked away.

The doctor appeared on the doorstep and ushered her inside. He led the way through to the sitting-room and sat her down on an armchair.

'Could you eat lunch?' he asked her, and wasn't too surprised when she shook her head. The baby, however, began to cry slightly, a hungry cry, and the doctor suggested gently, 'You'd better feed him, lass, while I get us a cup of tea.'

He left the room and, unbuttoning her blouse, Riona put the baby to her breast. He drew on her milk, but for once she drew no comfort from his closeness. She was still shaken by her encounter with Cameron.

The baby was fed by the time the doctor returned with a tray of tea things. Riona put him down on the carpet and he lay there happily, trying but not quite managing to roll over. She felt calmer herself, already distancing her mind and her heart from Cameron Adams, as she'd done once before.

'I'm sorry, lass,' the doctor said when he'd served the tea, 'I'm an interfering old man. I just thought . . . well, if the two of you got together, you might make up your differences.'

Riona shook her head. 'As you probably noticed, Doctor, he hates me.'

'Och, no,' Dr Macnab denied, 'he doesna hate you, lass. It's jealousy that's driving him. He's got some mad idea that you've been with Fergus as well as himself, and he can't stand it.'

Clearly the doctor didn't believe Cameron's accusations, and Riona could have left him with his illusions. But that was what she'd done with Cameron. She'd let him imagine her totally innocent and it had resulted in disaster.

This time she decided to be honest. 'I have, Doctor.'

'You have what, lass?' Dr Macnab didn't realise she was answering him.

'I have been with Fergus,' she stated plainly.

Still the doctor doubted what she was trying to say. 'Well, of course, lass,' he agreed. 'As I remember, Fergus was a great deal of help to you on his last leave, when your grandfather was ill. But that hardly has you sleeping with him, as Cameron thinks. You've never felt that way about Fergus, have you, lass?' he ended with certainty.

'No, I never really loved Fergus,' she told him quietly, 'but that's what makes it worse. Because, you see . . . I did sleep with him, Doctor,' she finally confessed, raising her eyes to his, so he could read the truth in them.

'Och, no, lass.' Dr Macnab didn't want to believe what she was telling him. 'You're no saying Cameron was right—that you were sleeping with both of them?'

Riona shook her head. 'Not the way he meant it.' She recalled his words with a mixture of anger and pain. 'I slept with Fergus just the once—a week or so after my grandfather's funeral. He'd been so good to me, so kind, and I felt so alone. I thought I loved him. I wanted to. I guess I was scared of having no one.'

'I understand, lass.' Dr Macnab was quick to support her. 'Don't blame yourself. It happens sometimes. You won't be the first person to have turned to the nearest person in grief.'

'I suppose it was that.' She nodded. 'I felt guilty, too. He'd helped so much around the place. At first it was just as a friend, but then he said he was in love with me. I don't think now he was . . . I just wanted to believe it. At any rate, we did sleep together,' she admitted, more ashamed of the fact than she'd ever been of her relationship with Cameron.

'Don't be so hard on yourself, lass.' Dr Hamish squeezed her hand gently. 'Roddy had just died and you were confused and depressed and perhaps a little scared of being on your own. You were vulnerable and Fergus took advantage.'

Riona shook her head. She didn't think it fair to blame Fergus. 'We used each other, Doctor. I was relieved when he returned to sea and he was happy to go. I think we both knew we weren't really suited. He never wrote and it was a surprise when he turned up that night.'

'It was Cameron who gave him the lift here.' The doctor recalled what the American had said.

'Apparently.' Riona's eyes became shadowed. 'I didn't know it then. Fergus just told me he'd hitched a lift from a tourist, and Cameron... well, I never saw him again.'

'I remember. He left very suddenly.' The doctor frowned, as he concluded, 'Presumably because he found out about you and Fergus.'

'I suppose.' Riona wasn't altogether sure; perhaps he'd just used it as an excuse. If he'd really loved her, wouldn't he have given her a chance to explain? 'Except there was nothing to find out, not that time,' she declared a little angrily, 'because all Fergus and I did was talk. I told him there was someone else and, though he was angry, he accepted it. I let him spend the night there because it was too late for him to go home, but, whatever Cameron Adams thinks, Fergus spent it on the couch. Believe me, Doctor, we didn't——'

'I do,' the older man was quick to assure. 'You don't have to convince me, lass. But you can see how it must have looked to Cameron—Fergus returns and you go back with him, just like Isobel suggested. If only he'd known the truth. Maybe if you told him now——'

'No!' Riona stopped the doctor from saying more. If there had ever been a chance for her and Cameron, it was gone.

'But why not?' Dr Macnab still hoped for a happy ending.

'He chose to believe the worst,' Riona reasoned, 'because he wanted to. He wanted to ditch me, and I just made it easy for him.'

'No, lass, no.' The doctor saw no logic in what she was saying. 'The man was mad with jealousy. He still is. Why would he want to ditch you?'

Riona shook her head, not wishing to discuss the matter further. It wouldn't change the past, and she had to look to the future. The future was the baby who reached out his little arms to her from the floor. She picked him up and cradled his dark head to her.

The doctor watched the two of them together, and asked, 'What are you going to do, lass?'

'I don't know, Doctor,' she admitted heavily. 'I don't want to marry him, yet what he's offering Rory...'

'Aye, it's some dowry,' Dr Hamish sighed, 'though he's expecting you to pay the price. No remarriage until Rory's grown.'

The latter didn't worry Riona. She didn't visualise meeting someone else she might want to marry. It was the rest of the package that was hard to accept. A move to Boston, however temporary, and undoubted resentment from a family who had no knowledge of his 'bride'. Then a return to Scotland to be installed as the lady of Invergair Hall. Once she might have managed both, with Cameron's love. Without it, she had the courage to face neither.

But what choice did she have? Face a court battle which she wasn't too certain of winning? Turn her back on all Cameron could give their son? She had only love, and it wasn't enough. In a few years Rory would see what others had and know what he lacked. And perhaps he would find out what could have been his for the taking. How would she feel then? How would she feel when another pair of dark blue eyes looked at her with scorn?

She shut her own eyes in pain at the idea and tightly held the baby who was now her whole life.

CHAPTER SIX

RIONA stared out of the aeroplane window although there was nothing to see but white cloud. Soon they would land. She paled at the thought. Would anyone be there to meet them? Would his family? She assumed he had told them of the child and prospective bride he was bringing home. How had they reacted?

It was almost two weeks since he'd made his absurd proposition. For several days she'd done nothing but wait in dread for a solicitor's letter to drop through her letter-box. Then Rory had fallen ill. Dr Macnab had diagnosed a simple virus but had warned her that the baby might be prone to respiratory ailments. To be on the safe side, he had transferred Rory to the cottage hospital.

Riona knew then she could never bring Rory back to the crofthouse. The estate had done essential repairs in the last year, but the damp in the walls had proved impossible to eradicate. It wasn't hard to envisage how that seeping damp would affect Rory's health in the winter.

She sat by her son's cot in the little hospital and searched for a way out. She saw only one. She went up to Invergair Hall the next morning.

With little sleep and in a confused but determined state, she'd barged her way past Mrs Mackenzie, the housekeeper, tracked down Cameron to the breakfast table, and announced without preamble, 'All right, I'll do it.'

'Do what?' A disconcerted Cameron lowered the newspaper he'd been reading.

'I'll marry you,' she stated plainly, 'under the conditions you stipulated . . . assuming you still want me to.'

'I . . . of course.' He rose from the table, his eyes questioning her sanity for a moment, before switching to Mrs Mackenzie in the doorway.

The housekeeper, having tried and failed to stop Riona at the front door, had followed in her wake. Now she stood open-mouthed at what she'd just heard.

With some of his usual composure, Cameron said, 'Perhaps you could make us a fresh pot of coffee, Mrs Mackenzie?'

The housekeeper stared open-mouthed for a second longer, before nodding, 'Aye . . . yes, sir,' and backing out of the room.

'Would you like to sit down?' he invited Riona. 'Or are there any more dramatic pronouncements to come?'

Riona's lips thinned. She hadn't meant to be dramatic. She'd just meant to get it over with. She hadn't planned on having Mrs MacKenzie as witness, and, consequently, the whole of Invergair, but it was something she'd have to live with.

'No, there's no more.' She ignored the seat he drew out for her. 'We can go when Rory gets better. He's sick at the moment,' she added in a flat tone that hid the guilt she felt.

'Yes, I know,' Cameron revealed. 'Macnab told me. Has his illness anything to do with your decision?'

Riona hunched her shoulders. 'Maybe. Does it matter?'

'Not particularly.' The chill returned to his tone even as he stated, 'I should be able to get a special licence in a couple of days. I assume Archibald, the minister, will agree to marry us. Dr Macnab, I'm sure, will be happy to give you away.'

Riona shuddered at the idea and shook her head. 'I've agreed to marry you and I will. But I won't do it here in Invergair.'

'Is that so?' His face set in hard lines. 'Perhaps you'd care to give a reason.'

'I...well, to be honest, it would be too embarrassing,' Riona admitted frankly.

'I see.' His voice was now like ice. 'You find the prospect of marrying me in public humiliating.'

'I never said that.' Riona felt he was deliberately twisting her words. She'd simply meant that marrying him with all Invergair looking on would be something of an ordeal. 'Anyway, the deal was I marry you to legitimise Rory. I can do that in Boston.'

'Ensuring any embarrassment is mine,' he countered.

Riona frowned. 'Yours?'

'If we marry in Boston, my family will expect to attend,' he pointed out, leaving Riona to conclude that, as a bride, she was going to be something of a disappointment to them.

Her green eyes darkened with temper, but she controlled it. They had six long months ahead of them and, to survive it, she would have to learn indifference. She had already accepted that in Boston she would be regarded, and possibly treated, as a nobody.

'Still, if that's your only condition.' Cameron conceded the matter with a shrug, before drily adding, 'At any rate, our marrying won't remain a secret round Invergair very long. Not unless Mrs Mackenzie exercises considerable restraint.'

Riona doubted that, but she'd just have to put up with the gossip and speculation when she returned from America. Anything was better than standing up in front of the minister who had baptised her and lying her way through a marriage ceremony, promising to love and cherish a man she now felt only bitterness towards.

'So, as soon as Rory's better,' he continued at her silence, 'we'll travel to the States.'

'Yes, all right.' Riona's emotionless tones hid the dread she felt. In other circumstances going to Boston might have seemed an adventure, but in these it was more like a prison sentence she had to serve to secure her son's future.

* * *

A week later they departed. Rory had been given the all-clear by Dr Macnab, and she had been given his blessing too. A romantic at heart, the old doctor imagined that they were one step away from reconciliation, and he had just smiled knowingly when Riona had explained it was only a temporary arrangement, her going to Boston.

If he had been with them on the journey, Riona felt sure the doctor would have realised the true situation. They had driven from Invergair to Inverness, flown to London, taken Concorde to New York, then the hourly shuttle from New York to Boston. A whole day together, and they'd barely exchanged a word.

On every flight Cameron sat aloof from them both. They didn't need to talk, so they didn't. She followed where he led, getting off one plane on to another, relying on the stewardess announcements to discover the duration and destination of each flight. Occasionally she disappeared to breast-feed Rory in a washroom, but Cameron never asked where she was going and she didn't tell him.

Now they were circling Logan International Airport in preparation to land, and Riona began wishing she'd at least asked some basic questions. Like how had he explained Rory's existence to his family? And how had they reacted? Were they prepared to welcome Rory, if not her? She couldn't imagine they'd be pleased to have her around, even on a temporary basis, and they wouldn't have to be very perceptive to notice Cameron wasn't pleased, either.

He didn't hide the fact. She'd caught him watching her several times during the trip, with a hard unrelenting look on his face. And, behind that look, she could almost hear his brain clicking with cold precision, calculating how soon they could marry, then separate.

Riona bore his stare in stoical silence, and saw it change when his eyes moved to their son. He could so easily have felt the same resentment towards Rory, a child he hadn't planned on, had tried to prevent, but it was clear he didn't. He'd claimed him readily enough, right from the first moment of discovery, and he watched him now with all the pride of a new father. He was taking him back home to America, regardless of any problems it caused.

And there were going to be problems, Riona realised, as she thought once more of his family. He had told her they would stay in his father's and stepmother's house. His one-bedroom apartment wasn't large enough to accommodate them all. She assumed his parents had agreed to this arrangement, but that didn't mean they were happy about having a total stranger thrust upon them. And Rory, although a grandson to Charles Adams, was no blood relation to Barbara, Cameron's stepmother, or Melissa, his stepsister.

Well, she'd discover their feelings soon enough, Riona sighed, as the plane taxied along the runway and she realised the play was about to commence. If she wanted to survive its six-month run, then strong and tough and careless was what she had to be. And she could be all of those for her son.

They left the plane, Cameron carrying Rory in his seat, and she walked with head high through the crowd welcoming arrivals. She scanned the faces, waiting for someone to approach them. No one did and she released the breath she'd been holding. Cameron made arrangements at a desk for their luggage to follow them, then they walked out of the terminal building into the coolness of early evening.

Riona assumed they would hail a taxi and she did a double take when a large black limousine drew up before them. A uniformed chauffeur climbed out, hesitated a split second when he saw Riona and baby, then quickly recovered his professional manner as he opened the rear doors and took their hand luggage.

'Welcome home, Mr Adams,' he said, as Cameron ushered her in first.

'Thank you, Stevens,' Cameron acknowledged the greeting briefly.

Then the chauffeur, seeing their only remaining piece of luggage, offered automatically, 'Shall I take your...the baby, sir?'

'No, that won't be necessary. He'll travel in the rear with us,' Cameron relayed, and, so saying, skirted the car and strapped Rory into the seat on the far side.

Already installed in the car, Riona watched Stevens hover in attendance. Presumably the chauffeur normally relieved his employer of such menial tasks, but this situation was a new one to him. No one had told him to expect a baby in tow.

When Cameron was finished, he came round the car again, and climbed in beside Riona. She inched away automatically, but needn't have bothered. The back seat could have accommodated another person on its soft, plush leather, and had enough legroom to make a race-horse feel comfortable.

As they pulled away from the airport, Cameron flicked a switch and instructed, 'Drive to my apartment first, please, Stevens.'

The glass screen between front and rear remained in place, the message communicated by an internal microphone. The chauffeur came back with an immediate, 'Yes, sir,' before Cameron flicked off the switch.

Riona tried and failed to hide her stupefaction. Even at their closest, the most he'd ever told her was his family ran a construction business. She'd imagined a firm of builders, perhaps twenty or thirty, which he managed as his father's deputy. But somehow she didn't think that, even in America, moderately successful builders could afford shiny black limousines and scrupulously polite chauffeurs.

'What's wrong?' He watched the frown deepen on her forehead.

'Is this your car?' she asked, a tremor of anger in her voice.

'Technically, no,' he responded. 'The car and chauffeur are at my disposal as an executive of the Harcourt Adams Corporation.'

It took Riona just a moment to see through this careful phrasing. 'But your father owns the Harcourt Adams Corporation?'

'Only a percentage,' he corrected, without going on to admit how much.

Riona didn't ask. She already suspected Cameron Adams and his family came into the seriously rich category. She didn't want to pursue the subject in case he thought her interested in his wealth. Presumably that was why he'd kept so quiet about it last summer.

They drove in silence away from the airport, passing through a tunnel under Boston Harbour, before heading into central Boston. Eventually Stevens pulled up outside a large brick building where a uniformed doorman hovered.

'I won't be long,' Cameron stated coolly, not offering her the choice of seeing his flat, and, with a 'Circle the block' to Stevens, returned the doorman's smile of recognition with a nod.

They circled the block as suggested and Riona didn't need much experience to know from the impressive façade of Victorian town houses that they were in one of the more prestigious areas of downtown Boston. The shops were of the exclusive variety—little designer dress shops and canopied restaurants, discreet jewellers and small galleries offering original paintings. Riona wondered where residents shopped for food, or did they just perpetually eat out?

She caught Stevens looking at her in the mirror and offered him a wry smile to match her thoughts. She was pleasantly surprised when his stiff features cracked a little into an answering smile. At least the family servants might be prepared to be pleasant to her.

They were circling round the block a third time when Cameron reappeared with a couple of cases. Stevens drew to a halt and leapt out to open doors and stow away the extra luggage.

They continued westwards, out of the city, through the borough of Arlington, heading for Lexington, names Riona recalled from books she'd read, then turned off into a residential area of wide avenues and large houses, each bigger than the last, until they finally stopped before a pair of iron gates set in a high brick wall. The gates opened automatically, and glided silently shut behind them.

Riona felt almost panicked, as if the shutting gates had made a prisoner of her. She felt no better when she looked ahead of her, at the house that lay at the end of the driveway. It wasn't so much a house as a mansion, fairly modern in age, three storeys high and sprawling outwards.

She turned and caught Cameron watching her again. His cynical expression suggested he thought her impressed by the grandness of his family home.

'I suppose you built it yourselves,' she said flatly.

He shook his head. 'Not quite. My father employed an architect, but only to incorporate his own ideas of house design. Hence the vague appearance of a shopping mall.'

'You don't like it?' she concluded from his tone.

He shrugged, as if his opinion was irrelevant. 'I suggest you let me do the talking,' he said, a thinly veiled order, as Stevens opened the passenger door.

Riona didn't argue. Dreading this first meeting with his family, she didn't imagine she'd want to say anything. She followed him out off the car, and started round the other side to unstrap the baby car-seat.

Cameron intercepted her. 'Rory's asleep. Perhaps it would be better if you left him. Stevens will look after him,' he directed at the hovering chauffeur.

'Ah...yes, sir.' Stevens didn't argue either.

Riona was reluctant, but she saw it might be simpler to meet the rest of the family, without Rory in tow.

'Could you please come and get me, if he wakes?' she asked the chauffeur.

'Certainly, miss...mam...' he stumbled awkwardly over her title. Clearly he hadn't a clue who she was.

Riona assumed things would be different inside the house, but the door was opened by a maid who also stared at her for a puzzled moment, before issuing a formal welcome to Cameron.

She informed him the family were in the lounge and Cameron crossed the marble hall with Riona in his wake. He opened one of the many doors off it and stepped inside the room. She hovered a few paces behind, shy and wary of meeting his family.

Voices died away at their entrance and for a moment the three people already seated in the room remained frozen where they were. The man, presumably Cameron's father although there was little resemblance, looked first to his son, a half-smile already forming on his lips. The two women glanced at him briefly before their eyes slid to Riona, calculating, assessing, dismissing.

Riona's gaze switched between all of them. Charles Adams, slighter and more thin-faced than Cameron, was still a handsome man, silver-haired and distinguished, with a wry expression that suggested he was glad to see his son.

Barbara Adams was surprisingly young-looking for a woman in her fifties, with auburn hair and stretched but unlined skin; she wore a plain black dress that did not detract from the exquisite diamond necklace round her neck. She also wore a look of icy disdain as she took in Riona.

Last but not least was Melissa Adams. With black hair, perfect features and perfect skin, she looked like a young Elizabeth Taylor. She wore black evening trousers and a colourful silk shirt which floated loosely round her slim frame. Neither her beauty nor her taste could be denied, and, as she looked Riona up and down, the

Scottish girl felt both large and plain in her cotton blouse and skirt.

Eventually Charles Adams rose from his chair and crossed to give Cameron a hard, masculine hug. 'Good to have you home, son,' he said with obvious affection before he glanced past him to the girl at his shoulder. 'And you must be Riona. It's a pleasure to meet you.'

'Thank you.' Riona, surprised at what appeared to be a genuine welcome, came forward and shyly offered her hand.

He took it and shook it warmly. 'How was the journey from Scotland?'

'Long,' Riona replied with a slight smile, and drew an indulgent look in return.

'Yes, you must be exhausted,' Charles Adams concluded and, turning to his wife, ran on, 'So, let's get the introductions over. This is Barbara, my wife, and my daughter, Melissa.'

Obliged to come forward, Barbara stood and offered a limp hand to Riona. They shook briefly. Melissa stood, too, but remained where she was, confining herself to a chilly smile.

Silence fell for a moment, an awkward, strained silence as neither of the women uttered any greeting and Riona followed suit. Then Charles Adams continued, 'Barbara's prepared some rooms for you and . . . and the baby.' He glanced in enquiry at Cameron.

He supplied, 'He's asleep in the car, Dad. Do you want to see him?'

'Do I want to see him?' his father repeated with a chuckle. 'My first grandchild, and he asks, "Do I want to see him?"'

It was clear Charles Adams couldn't wait to see Rory and Riona warmed to him. That Rory had appeared rather unconventionally seemed to make little difference to the older man, as he said, 'I still can't get over it,' and clasped Cameron by the shoulder in a gesture of congratulations and pride.

'Then come and meet him,' Cameron suggested and, exchanging smiles with his father, led the way out to the hall.

Barbara Adams gave Riona the briefest glance, a cold-eyed scrutiny, before following in her husband's wake.

Riona hesitated to join the family party. Although she was Rory's mother, she felt at the moment rather incidental. She took half a step towards the door, before a voice called her back. 'I'd leave them to it, if I were you. Unless, of course, you're into the excruciatingly sentimental.'

'Not particularly.' Riona turned to Melissa Adams, who had resumed her seat and was sipping her cocktail. Clearly Rory held no interest for her.

'No, somehow I didn't think you would be,' the American woman drawled on, and her tone made every word an insult. 'You can be sure my stepfather will be suitably impressed by your offspring, whatever it's like. While my dear mother will doubtless be hovering with a hypo.'

Riona, promising herself to keep as cool as the other girl, couldn't help being drawn by the latter.

'A hypo?' she echoed.

And Melissa Adams added patronisingly. 'You know, hypodermic. Used for taking blood. Which, in turn, can be used for genetic fingerprinting. You have heard of genetic fingerprinting, I assume?'

Riona gave a brief nod. She was well aware where the conversation was leading. She just wasn't going to help Melissa Adams get there.

'Then you'll know it can be used to conclusively establish fatherhood,' the American girl added, her dark eyes slanting like a cat's.

This time Riona didn't answer at all, but put on a look of studied boredom.

Melissa looked surprised, as if she expected more of a reaction—either tears or abuse from such an unsophisticated opponent. She had Riona pegged as scheming but stupid.

'Not that I doubt Cameron's paternity for a moment,' Melissa continued at length. 'Like any man, Cameron is capable of being driven entirely by his sexual urges, but out of bed he's not such a fool. In fact, I'm willing to bet he's already had the test done.'

'Actually, no, he didn't bother.' Riona somehow matched the other woman's calm. 'There was no need. You see Rory, *our* son, is the living image of his father.'

It was the first time Riona had taken pleasure in boasting of the fact. She'd done so because she knew such a likeness would hurt the other girl, who was plainly as jealous as a cat. She also knew that if she didn't fight back, Melissa Adams would make every second of her time in Boston a misery.

As it was, Melissa's cool façade had quickly changed to the spiteful manner that lay beneath. 'You think you've got him, don't you? But don't kid yourself. It'll take more than some bastard brat to hold on to Cam.'

'Really,' Riona said with studied dignity. 'Should I assume you are speaking from some vested interest?'

Melissa's lips thinned even more. She had thought Riona would be an easy conquest. Finding she wasn't, she lost her temper and any subtlety with it.

'If I want Cam, I just have to lift a finger.' Melissa's face turned ugly with anger. 'You won't make any difference. You'll see.'

'If you say so.' Riona affected indifference before turning on her heel and going out into the hall. There she took a deep breath to rid her head of the other girl's unpleasantness.

She saw the rest of the family standing at the front door. Charles Adams was holding a now wakened Rory and the two—grandfather and grandson—were getting to know each other. Rory seemed quite happy in another male stranger's arms; perhaps he could read the adoration so transparent on his grandfather's face. Barbara

Adams stood apart from them, her lips compressed into a thin line; obviously she wasn't overjoyed at this small addition to the family.

Cameron glanced towards Riona, his eyes questioning where she'd been. She responded with a small, thin smile as she wondered how he would react if he knew of the little tête-à-tête she'd had with his stepsister. She couldn't imagine him taking her side, at any rate.

Riona walked forward and Rory's head switched round at the sound of her footsteps on the marble hall. He gave a brief cry at the sight of his mother and Charles had the wisdom to hand him over. He nestled himself against Riona's neck, the bond clear for all to see.

Charles Adams smiled at the picture, and said with gratitude, 'He's the image of Cameron as a baby.'

Riona smiled back, glad of at least one ally in the house.

When Barbara Adams finally spoke up, her tone was cold and practical as she informed them, 'I've given Miss Macleod and the child the nursery quarters. Cameron I've put in his usual room.'

'But they're in opposite wings,' Charles Adams objected to the arrangements.

'That's all right, Dad.' Cameron had no desire to be nearer Riona, but he couldn't resist mocking his stepmother with a dry, 'And should we presume you'll be patrolling the corridors as well, Barbara? Or are appearances preserved with separate quarters?'

Barbara Adams scowled openly at her stepson. 'We all know you've never cared what people think of you, Cameron. However, your father and I have a position to keep up in this town. It will be embarrassing enough to account for the sudden materialisation of a six-month-old baby, without giving our servants more to gossip about to our friends' servants.'

'Oh, things aren't that bad, Barbara,' Charles Adams chided her a little, feeling she was overstating the case. 'I'm not sure anybody cares much these days about that sort of thing. Anyway, Cameron and Riona can be married in a month, set up in their own home, and who'll remember what in a couple of years? Right, son?' He smiled at Cameron for support.

Cameron's expression was wry, as he echoed, 'Right, Dad.'

It was Riona who felt uncomfortable. For some reason Charles Adams had accepted her as his future daughter-in-law, instead of judging her as not good enough, as she'd expected. She felt guilty when she planned to stick around only long enough for the ink to dry on a marriage certificate.

Charles caught her unhappy expression and misunderstood, adding quickly, 'Of course, the choice of wedding and home is up to Riona.'

'To a limited degree,' Barbara Adams interceded. 'I mean, she can hardly sail down the aisle in clouds of white lace, now can she?' The older woman's eyes slid to Riona with barely veiled contempt for her and the baby that made a white wedding a mockery.

Riona just stared back, realising she'd have to grow a second skin to survive the women of this house. 'Don't worry. Five minutes in a Register Office will do me.'

'Surely not,' Charles appealed to both her and Cameron. 'So you've jumped the gun a little. Lots of couples do these days. It doesn't mean you can't have a day to remember all your lives. And Riona will make the most beautiful bride, don't you think, Cameron?'

Cameron neither agreed nor disagreed, saying instead, 'It's up to her.'

Riona shot him an ill-disguised look of hostility. He must know she didn't want any grand ceremony. It was up to him to scotch the idea.

'For now, I think we'll go and freshen up,' he added, catching the look and deciding not to rely on Riona's acting abilities for much longer.

'Yes, sure, son. You go up and get settled, and we'll put a hold on dinner,' Charles assured, as Cameron took Riona's arm and began to steer her up the staircase.

Out of the corner of her eye, Riona caught sight of Melissa leaning in the lounge doorway, watching their progress upstairs. She was awarded a look of malice from the girl. Cameron noticed, and raised a questioning brow. Riona ignored it, continuing up the broad staircase.

They remained silent even when they reached the upper gallery, out of view, and walked along a lengthy corridor, then down another, before they reached the rooms that had once been used as nursery quarters. The rooms were isolated from the main part of the house, a fact that actually pleased Riona.

She looked round what would be Rory's bedroom. An antique wooden cot had been retrieved from somewhere and placed beside a single bed. The wallpaper was teddy bears on a background of pink. The carpeting was pink, too.

'Who last used it?' Riona asked out of curiosity.

'Melissa,' Cameron answered evenly. 'She was just two when my father married Barbara and they came to this house.'

'Your mother didn't live here,' Riona concluded out loud.

He shook his head and gave a brief laugh. 'My mother would never have wanted to live anywhere like this. When I was young, we lived in an apartment in Boston near the park. It was quite big, but it wasn't showy.'

It was clear which he preferred, and Riona deduced that the more showy mansion was his stepmother's choice. She imagined it must have been hard on him, losing his mother at eight, losing the home they'd shared at thirteen. For a moment her heart went out to the boy he'd been, then she stifled an emotion that threatened to make her soft.

His face closed up, too, perhaps regretting any confidences, as he led the way through to the adjoining bedroom. It was carpeted, with a wardrobe, single bed and dressing-table, functional rather than luxurious, but adequate for Riona's needs.

It was Cameron who looked round the basic room and said, 'This was the nanny's room. You won't have to stay here. I'll get you moved to somewhere better.'

Riona shook her head. 'It'll do me. It's no worse than the crofthouse.'

'No, I don't suppose so,' Cameron agreed, and for a moment their eyes met and held, thinking the same thoughts, remembering a time when neither cared nor even noticed the dilapidated state of her crofthouse. They'd been too absorbed in each other.

Riona felt her heart gripped painfully tight for a moment, and she dropped her eyes away. She sat down on the bed and laid Rory on the quilt cover.

'Anyway, I'll be all right,' she ran on, 'so if you want to go back and join your family, I don't mind.'

'Not particularly——' he pulled a face '—but I suppose I'll have to face the third degree some time... At least we seem to have pleased my father,' he added ironically.

Riona remembered the older man's delight and felt guilty. 'Yes, well... don't you think you should tell him the truth?'

'And which truth would that be?' Cameron enquired on a sardonic note.

'That we're not planning on staying married,' she reminded him heavily. 'That we're simply doing it for Rory's sake.'

He shook his head. 'The agreement was we marry and at least pretend to the outside world to make a go of it.'

'To the people in Invergair, yes,' she agreed, 'but surely you don't want to deceive your family?'

'I know my father. He will prefer to believe I'm settling down for real, even if it's only for six months. My stepmother, she won't care either way.'

'And Melissa?' Riona couldn't help slipping the girl's name in, watching for a reaction.

'Melissa?' His eyes narrowed on her, questioning what she knew and what she didn't. 'Why should it be of interest to Melissa?'

Riona's lips thinned. Did he think he had to hide his relationship with his stepsister from her? Did he imagine she'd react with the same spiteful jealousy?

'Did Mel say anything to you?' he queried at her silence.

'When?' Riona responded, deliberately obtuse.

'Earlier, when the rest of us went out to Rory,' he stated impatiently.

'Oh, you know, just girl talk,' she answered with aggravating vagueness.

He scowled, before suggesting coldly, 'I wouldn't take too much notice of what Mel says. In fact, if you're wise, you'll stay out of her way.'

Riona had no intention of furthering her acquaintance with his malicious stepsister, but she was sure his advice didn't come from any desire to protect *her*. Rather he wanted to keep the two women apart for his own reasons—like the fact, maybe, that Melissa was right—that, given a choice, he would have been walking down the aisle with the American girl, and maybe still planned such a future.

'Don't worry, I won't spoil things for you,' Riona responded dourly, and drew a frown for her trouble.

But he chose not to challenge the remark and instead said, 'Right, I'll go down now. Leave you to change.'

'Change?' Riona echoed.

'For dinner,' he reminded her.

She gave a short laugh. Back on his own home territory, he seemed to have forgotten the reality of hers.

'Change into what?' She glanced down at her plain cotton shirt and skirt. 'Our luggage isn't here yet and, anyway, I'm already wearing my best.'

He looked over her crumpled clothing, and clearly found her wanting. Last summer he had never noticed, or, at least, never cared what she wore.

'I should have realised,' he muttered now, 'taken you to a few shops when we were in London.'

Riona shrugged. It didn't bother her. She didn't want him dressing her up to fit in with his lifestyle.

She said, 'It doesn't matter. The truth is I'd prefer to dine up here.'

Perhaps he heard the weariness in her voice, because he didn't argue. 'Yeah, OK, I suppose I could plead jet-lag on your behalf and get something sent up here to-night,' he conceded.

'Fine,' she accepted shortly.

She managed to sound tough and uncaring, while inside she already felt the terrible loneliness that would be hers for the next six months. She kept her face blank of expression, rather than betray any weakness.

'Nothing ever fazes you, does it, Riona?' Cameron remarked with reluctant admiration. 'Nothing ever really touches you.'

If he wanted to think that, Riona didn't mind. She wasn't about to tell him that his leaving last summer had more than fazed her, more than touched her. It had left her heart breaking.

She remained silent, and picked up Rory from the bed. He was beginning to become fretful, making familiar hungry sounds. She directed an impatient look at Cameron, willing him gone.

He caught it, and, with a mutter of, 'I'll have some dinner sent up,' went out the way they'd come in, through the nursery.

When he'd left, Riona unbuttoned her blouse and put the baby to her breast. He fed contentedly, his eyes gazing up at her in perfect love and trust. She kissed his soft forehead, and reminded herself it was to secure his future she was here, but even Rory in her arms couldn't dispel her sense of being alone.

Sadness crept over her, and she barely heard a knock on the corridor door. By the time she called, 'No, don't——' the door had already opened and her visitor was standing on the threshold. It was Cameron returned, and her first emotion was relief that it had been no one else.

Relief, however, gave away to embarrassment, as Cameron's eyes went from her face to the breast on which his son was feeding. She would have covered herself, but she had nothing to cover herself with, and to abruptly stop the feed would distress Rory. So she sat where she was, nursing her baby, and hoped Cameron would respect her privacy and leave.

Instead he shut the door behind him, and continued to stare at her and his son, and this special bond between them. On another man, the look on his face might have been wonder at the first sight of his woman breastfeeding their child. On Cameron, who knew what thoughts lay behind his steady blue gaze?

He stood there watching, as if he had every right to, as if it were the most natural thing in the world, until the baby eventually fell asleep on the breast, and Riona gently detached him, and, laying him down on the bed, re-buttoned her clothes.

'I didn't realise you were feeding him yourself,' Cameron said, still in no hurry to leave.

She nodded. 'It's best, when they're very young,' she stated factually, before picking Rory up and carrying him through to the nursery.

Cameron watched from the doorway as she settled Rory in the cot. The baby snuffled a little, but remained asleep. Riona switched on a small night-light before backing quietly out of the room.

Cameron remained where he was, and Riona put some space between them by crossing to the window.

'I came back to ask you what Rory would need in the way of food,' he explained his own reappearance, then,

with the trace of a smile, added, 'but I can see you have
that under control.'

'Yes.' For some reason Riona chose that moment to
blush like a rose.

She lowered her head, hoping the curtain of her blonde
hair might hide it, but he saw, and, more, saw deep inside
her. 'You're still just a kid, Ree, aren't you?' His voice
and manner softened. 'You might have a smart mouth
and a hard head, and a baby at your breast, but, underneath, you'll still the tomboy kid I met last year on the
road to Invergair.'

'No, I'm not!' she denied automatically, then child-
ishly snapped, 'And don't call me Ree! I hate it.'

'You never said.' It was the pet name he had used for
her from their first night together. 'But then you never
said a lot of things, did you? Like you weren't the virgin
I took you for... Did you think I'd have cared?' he demanded, his voice harshening.

'I don't know.' Riona couldn't explain why she hadn't
told him, and she didn't want to go over it now. 'Does
it matter? It's past. Forgotten...'

'Not by me it isn't.' His eyes reflected the bitterness
he felt. 'Part of me wanted you and had to have you,
but another part felt as if I was spoiling something
perfect. I promised you the earth to make up for it, and
all the time you were leading me on. All the time you
were just keeping it warm for your sailor boy.'

'I... that's disgusting!' Riona hissed back. 'It wasn't
like that. I didn't know Fergus was going to turn
up——'

'You think that makes it better? You let him sail right
back into port, didn't you?' he accused crudely.

'That's not true!' Riona's fingers curled into the palms
of her hands. 'You've twisted everything. If you'd just
come and asked me about Fergus, instead of *spying* on
me——'

'Oh, yeah, I could have asked you,' he echoed with
a rancorous laugh. 'And what convincing little story

would you have made up? Don't tell me, he had to stay because he missed his last bus home.'

He said it knowing there was no local bus service in the Invergair area. The truth, however, wasn't so far from his mockery. Fergus had stayed because it was too late to go home to his parents' house.

Riona saw there would be no point in trying to explain this to Cameron. He didn't want to listen. He wanted to believe the worst of her. It made her want to hurt him back.

'You know your trouble, Mr Bigshot Adams?' she sneered in reply. 'You can't stand the thought that I might have preferred Fergus to you. Despite your money and your flash car, I chose Fergus, and that sticks in your throat,' she said, damning herself forever, not caring, glad that he looked crippled by her words.

He responded in a growl, 'Well, neither of us got what we wanted in the end, did we? Tell me, what happened to sailor boy? Couldn't he take it when you had *my* bastard, not his?'

'Don't call Rory a bastard!' Riona cried back.

'Why? It's you who made him one,' he accused with hard contempt.

Riona flinched visibly, accepting the truth of what he'd said. If she'd taken his advice, there would have been no baby.

They stared at each other for a moment, the worst kind of enemies—the kind who had once been lovers—then he crossed to the door and departed without another word.

Riona continued to stare after him, anger dissipating, giving way to despair. Their brief love had turned into such a bitter thing. The only part of it left was Rory.

She went back through to the nursery and looked down at her sleeping baby and questioned if she really wanted him to bear the name of a man who hated her so much, wondered if she could stand pain like this inflicted daily. Then she thought once more of the hills of Invergair, purple with heather, yellow with bracken, wild in their grand beauty, and asked herself if she could do anything else. She could turn down such a prize for herself, but for her son?

She thought of what she had to offer. Love...love and nothing. A home with damp walls. A future on state benefits. Half a name as the laird's bastard child.

'I can do it,' she reassured the sleeping baby and herself. 'It's me he wants to hurt, not you. If I can just get through it, he'll give you everything.'

Riona didn't question that he would, for, despite everything, she still trusted the sense of honour and pride that were an essential part of Cameron's make-up. He had promised Invergair to Rory, and he would live up to that promise, if she lived up to hers.

Her mind wandered back to last summer and the gentler, kinder Cameron she would have married without a second thought. Then her mind returned to the present and the sham of a marriage they were to go through, and she knew that, even without Fergus's untimely reappearance, they had never been destined to live happily ever after.

She was what she was—a nobody, without the necessary money or sophistication or family name to enter his world as an equal. He was what he was—too wealthy, too experienced, too everything for the likes of her. And last summer?

Last summer had been only a dream.

CHAPTER SEVEN

RIONA slept fitfully and woke early as usual for Rory's first feed. She looked out of the window, judging it was going to be a warm day, and dressed in a light blue denim shirt and colourful cotton skirt that hung cool and loose round her. Then she remained in her room, wondering if someone would come and fetch her.

Eventually a maid appeared carrying a tray of breakfast things. With her was another girl who introduced herself shyly, 'I'm Gloria. My mother is cook here. Mr Adams—young Mr Adams—asked if I would help you with your baby.'

The girl had dark eyes and dark hair, and was what the Americans called Hispanic. She also had a lovely smile that she bestowed on Rory as she came to crouch on the floor where he was half sitting with a little support from Riona's leg.

Rory seemed to take to her straight away as she made clucking noises to attract his attention and offered him a finger to clutch hold off.

Riona took to the girl, too, although she said, 'That's kind of you, Gloria, but I can pretty well manage Rory on my own.'

'Mr Adams wished me to go shopping with you,' Gloria relayed. 'He says you need to buy clothes and things for the baby.'

Riona frowned. It was true. Rory had almost grown out of his first size of clothes and she had no pram or push-chair or toys for him. She just wished Cameron had discussed the matter with her first.

'We'll see.' Riona smiled at the girl; she had no quarrel with her. 'I'll speak to Mr Adams.'

She rose and picked up Rory as if to go and do just that, and Gloria said apologetically, 'I think he has already gone to work with his father.'

'Oh.' Riona looked at her watch; it had just gone eight.

'Stevens, the chauffeur, is to drive us into Boston,' Gloria explained, 'after you've had breakfast.'

'I...' Riona wanted to object to all these plans being made without her, but she caught the other's worried look and realised she was being unfair. Gloria was just a messenger, obeying her employer's instructions. 'I— all right,' Riona surrendered with a sigh, and asked, tongue in cheek, 'I don't suppose Mr Adams has told you specifically where I'm meant to shop?'

Gloria took her literally and gave a smiling nod. 'He suggested the big stores, like Filene's or Jordan Marsh. They all have baby departments. Mr Adams says you are to buy anything you want. He will arrange charging facilities.'

'I see.' Riona didn't really, but decided not to show her ignorance.

'If you wish, I will hold the baby while you have your breakfast.' Gloria indicated the tray of coffee and freshly baked rolls.

Riona hesitated for a fraction, then handed Rory over. He made a little cry of protest, but was soon distracted by Gloria as she made funny faces.

Gloria was clearly experienced with babies, and, when they did go on the proposed shopping expedition, she proved indispensable. She knew the right stores for the things they needed, knew where they might change Rory's nappy and where Riona might breast-feed him in comfort.

Without her encouragement, however, Riona might have spent a little less money. She might have gone for the medium-priced push-chair rather than the best on the market. She might have resisted the little jump suits that cost a ridiculous amount for a scrap of material. She might have decided that a six-month-old baby didn't need sophisticated babywalkers and cot toys and bouncers and a host of other goods. But it was too easy to say, 'Charge it to the Adams account,' to assistants happy to do so.

It was only when Stevens picked them up in the limousine, seemingly to take her to what he called the Harcourt Adams building, that she actually looked through the credit slips she'd been handed. Then she realised she'd spent what seemed like a small fortune in just a couple of hours. She wondered what Cameron would think: would he wonder perhaps if she'd really been a fortune-hunter all along?

As they drove, Gloria pointed out landmarks of the city: Boston Common and the public garden of botanical interest, then the John Hancock Building, the tallest structure in New England, with sixty floors and covered with plate glass that reflected the sky and other buildings around. Riona stared up in near awe at the size of it, while Gloria explained that at the top was an observatory that offered a panoramic view of the city. They had left behind the older more historical Boston of Beacon Hill, with its elegant old houses and prestigious family names, and arrived in the still expanding area of Back Bay, which boasted several skyscrapers and modern buildings of weird and wonderful design.

The Harcourt Adams building was, by some standards, quite modest. It boasted only twenty-five floors, and was built on symmetrical lines. However, it was so far from the small building firm Riona had visualised that she laughed at her naïveté. Whatever he'd claimed last summer, Cameron would surely never have given up this family empire for the lairdship of Invergair.

While Gloria remained in the car with Rory, Stevens escorted Riona inside. She trailed behind him, as he marched up to the two elegantly suited receptionists at the front desk and announced, 'Miss Macleod to see Mr Cameron Adams.'

To their credit, the receptionists didn't stare over long at Riona, just long enough for her to realise that, in her simple blue shirt and cotton skirt, she looked like neither family nor girlfriend nor business colleague. They quickly lowered raised eyebrows, masked any curiosity, and got on with the business of notifying Cameron of her presence.

After a brief exchange on the telephone, one of the receptionists informed Stevens, 'Miss Macleod is to wait in the reception area. Mr Adams will be down shortly.'

Stevens nodded at the information, then indicated to Riona the arrangement of plush chairs and coffee-tables in the large reception hall. Riona must have looked as awkward as she felt, hesitating over taking up any of the squashy leather armchairs, and Stevens impulsively offered, 'Do you wish me to wait with you, miss?'

Riona shook her head, but softened the refusal with a smile. It was clear the family chauffeur had seen right through her. She might be a prospective bride to the son of the house, but she was just an ordinary Scottish girl, unused to servants and limousines and plush reception areas in multi-million-pound businesses.

'If the baby cries, could you bring him to me, please?' she asked Stevens in a manner more polite than any of the family would use.

He responded with warmth, 'Certainly, miss. I'll get Gloria to carry the little fellow in,' before departing with a reassuring smile.

Aware of the receptionists' interest, Riona forced herself to sit on one of the leather armchairs and pick up one of the glossy magazines and try and look natural. She wondered if other girlfriends of Cameron, sleek long-legged brunettes or small sophisticated redheads, had frequented the same chairs, waiting for him. She pulled a face, then started as Cameron suddenly appeared before her. 'What's wrong?'

'Nothing.' She blushed slightly and covered her real thoughts by saying, 'I was just thinking how important you must be, running this place.'

'Not really.' Cameron shrugged in dismissal. 'My father runs it. I'm merely an executive.'

'But one day you'll run it,' Riona persisted, wondering why he was playing down his position.

He shook his head. 'It's not a simple matter of succession.'

Riona frowned. 'But if your father owns the company, then surely it'll be yours eventually.'

'My father owns thirty per cent of Harcourt Adams,' Cameron corrected in even tones. 'I own ten per cent, left to me by my grandfather. Barbara holds another forty per cent of the stock. The rest is divided up among small stockholders.'

'I don't understand,' Riona admitted openly. 'Why did your father give Barbara forty per cent of the company?'

'He didn't.' Cameron smiled grimly at such an idea. 'Barbara was a Harcourt before marriage. My grandfather and her father merged their respective businesses about twenty-five years ago.'

'Before your father married Barbara,' Riona concluded without much tact.

Cameron agreed cynically. 'Quite. You might say their marriage consolidated the merger.'

Riona wondered what that meant exactly. Had the marriage been more a matter of expediency than romance?

Cameron seemed to confirm it, as he went on, 'With control of the majority stockholding, my father secured the role of president when the older generation were gone.'

Riona began to understand. With his second wife's support, Charles Adams had well over half of the shares in his pocket. But what about the future? Could

Cameron count on his stepmother's support? Or, later, Melissa's?

Yes, if he married her... The thought crept into Riona's head, and refused to creep out again. It had to be the perfect match. Beautiful Melissa, handsome Cameron, and eighty per cent of Harcourt Adams between them.

'I suppose Melissa will inherit her mother's share,' Riona asked without much subtlety.

Cameron's eyes narrowed. 'I imagine so, yes... And yes to what you're thinking as well.'

'What I'm thinking?' Riona feigned innocence, but not very well.

'That should I marry Melissa——' he read her perfectly '—Harcourt Adams would be mine for the taking.'

Riona felt angry at being so transparent and snapped, 'You said it, not me!'

'Well, you can forget it,' he told her abruptly. 'I'm marrying you, whether you like it or not.'

Riona didn't. Not like this. He was marrying to give their son a name, and for no other reason. He was marrying her, when, in all likelihood, he would prefer to be marrying his beautiful stepsister. For a marriage of convenience, it didn't seem very convenient at all.

'Don't you want all this?' She looked round the plush reception hall, a symbol of the Harcourt Adams Corporation's success and importance.

'You mean power, prestige, wealth... Should I?' he countered enigmatically.

'I...' Riona looked at him, not knowing the answer, suddenly aware she didn't really know the man. His hopes, dreams, ambitions—what did he want from life?

'Never mind.' He left her in ignorance, and, taking her arm, muttered, 'Come on. We have a lot to do.'

'Why? Where are we going?' Riona asked as they walked towards the limousine.

'Lunch—unless you've already had it,' Cameron responded briefly.

Riona shook her head, but remained puzzled. Why would Cameron wish to take her to lunch?

He answered her frown, saying, 'We have things to discuss. A restaurant will afford us more privacy than my father's house.'

'I suppose,' Riona agreed, but gestured towards her skirt and shirt, 'Just don't make it anywhere too posh.' Cameron looked her up and down, and a deepening frown told her she definitely didn't pass inspection. It was small surprise when he himself was wearing a conservative dark suit, silk shirt and silk tie.

Riona, however, felt he didn't have to look quite so disapproving, or be quite so ready to agree with her, as he asked Stevens if he knew of any small, down-market restaurants in the area. Stevens, holding open the back door for the two of them, confirmed he did, and was soon criss-crossing back streets to reach their destination.

Gloria had discreetly moved to the front of the car to sit with Stevens. With the glass partition between, that left Cameron and Riona perfect privacy in the back. Cameron, however, seemed to have no desire to converse. He looked across her to his son, now asleep in his car-seat, then looked out at the passing streets. Riona, seated in the middle of the back seat, looked down at her hands and tried not to care about his indifference to her.

When they arrived at their destination, Cameron instructed Stevens and Gloria to wait in the car with Rory. Riona, if she felt like objecting to such an arrangement, wasn't given the chance, as he grasped her elbow and steered her inside the small Italian pizzeria.

With its polished wooden floor and pretty chequered tablecloths, it seemed to be a haunt of young student types. At any rate, she fitted in and Cameron didn't. He looked overdressed in his dark suit and drew a couple of stares from the more casually dressed clientele.

'Did you get all that you require for the baby?' he asked when they'd both given their order.

Riona nodded, then felt she should confess, 'I'm afraid I spent rather a lot.'

'Really?' Cameron raised an enquiring brow.

'I didn't mean to,' Riona ran on. 'I got carried away. There were so many nice things for babies.' She started to produce the credit slips that were burning a hole in her handbag.

He gestured for her to put them away. 'Just give us a ball-park figure,' he suggested drily.

'I... about a thousand dollars,' Riona finally admitted, rather shamefaced.

She waited for his reaction, and was startled when he laughed out loud.

'That much, hmm?' he commented with mock seriousness, then laughed again. 'You really have no idea, do you?'

'Of what?' Riona scowled now, realising he was laughing at her naïveté.'

'Money. Wealth. Life... Anything,' he summed up, his mouth still slanting with amusement. 'You practically have *carte blanche* to buy what you like, and you worry about spending a grand... Have you any idea what I'm worth?'

'No, and I don't want to,' Riona snapped in return. 'Not everyone's impressed by money, you know.'

'No, just nearly everyone,' Cameron commented cynically, but his sudden good humour remained as he continued, 'I don't suppose you spent anything on yourself.'

She shook her head, saying, 'There's nothing I need.'

'Think again.' His manner sobered as he informed her, 'A week on Friday my father and Barbara are throwing a small get-together for family and friends to meet the bride. When I say small, I mean only about thirty people. When I say get-together, I mean black tie and designer dress affair... Now, from memory, I don't think your wardrobe runs to formal dinner parties, and I assume you won't want to go in your jeans.'

'I don't care,' Riona claimed defiantly.

'Possibly you don't,' Cameron countered, 'but I do, so this afternoon we'll hit the dress shops.'

'We?'

'You and me.'

'You're joking.' Riona accepted she might need a suitable dress, but not with him as shopping companion. 'Don't you have any work to do?'

'Three desks full,' he confirmed, 'but it'll wait. Dressing you has priority.'

'How flattering.' Riona pulled a face, well aware he was only doing it so she wouldn't let him down totally.

He didn't have a chance to respond before the waiter appeared with their order, and Riona studiously concentrated on eating the pizza she'd requested.

She was almost finished when Gloria appeared in the restaurant with a wailing Rory in her arms. The wails subsided slightly as Riona took him, but he was clearly hungry.

'I have to feed him,' Riona informed Cameron, hoping he'd get the message. 'I'll go back to the car.'

To his credit, he understood immediately, saying, 'Send Stevens in to me.'

Riona duly did, before installing herself in the back seat of the spacious limousine and giving Rory her breast. She could do so in relative privacy as the darkened windows stopped prying eyes from outside. She did not count, however, on Cameron following her out to the car.

He climbed into the rear with her, sitting on the bench seat opposite, and, when she made a move to cover her breast, urged, 'Don't. I like to watch.'

Riona's face coloured at his frankness, but she did as he said, continuing to feed their child. She kept her head down, her loose blonde hair curtaining her face, but all the time she was conscious of Cameron's eyes on her and Rory, sucking hungrily on her breast. She knew it was the baby who held his interest, yet the feelings that stirred inside herself were for the man, and for a time not so long ago, when they had loved each other.

Perhaps he remembered too, for, when the baby finally released her nipple, a hand caught at hers before she could button back her shirt. Her eyes went to Cameron's, questioning the action, but his gaze was fixed on her breast, which was heavy and wet with milk. She had not thought of herself or her body as sensual since childbirth, but the look on his face suggested otherwise. When he raised his head, she saw her own desire reflected in his dark blue eyes.

Any protest caught in her throat as he leant towards her and she knew he was going to kiss her. She closed her eyes, wanting it, and felt the warmth of his breath on her cheek. Then suddenly the shrill sound of a police siren brought them both back to their senses. Riona's eyes flew open to catch a look of anger cross his face before he reached out and took Rory from her, muttering, 'Dress yourself.'

Riona did so, clumsily, now embarrassed by the whole incident. It was his fault. He should have kept his distance. Yet she was the one left feeling guilty.

They waited in silence for Stevens and Gloria, who were now having their lunch in the restaurant. Cameron continued to hold Rory, allowing him to pull on his silk tie, then giving him a set of keys to jangle. Although he wasn't demonstrative, Riona sensed Cameron's growing affection for his son. She looked away, detaching herself from the scene. They might seem the perfect, happy family, but it was a sham.

When the others returned, Cameron instructed Stevens to drive to the public gardens, explaining to her, 'I thought Gloria might walk Rory in the gardens while we shopped for clothes.'

'I have clothes,' Riona stated stubbornly.

'Yes, well...' he slid a critical eye over her denim blouse and loose cotton skirt '...clothes more suitable for your position.'

'Position? Position as what?' she challenged scornfully.

'My fiancée, naturally,' he declared in leaden tones.

Riona gave an inelegant snort of laughter. Did he really think dressing her up was going to fool anyone?

'I'm glad one of us is finding the situation amusing,' he responded icily, and Riona wondered once again what had happened to the warm, witty Cameron who had been able to laugh at himself in Invergair.

'I just don't see any point in pretending,' she sighed back, 'when everyone's going to know why you're marrying me. Dressing me up like a Barbie doll won't make any difference. I still won't be your sort.'

His lips thinned even more. 'Really? And what do you imagine is "my sort"?'

'I didn't mean yours specifically.' She wondered if he was deliberately misunderstanding her. He must know what she was getting at. 'I meant your family's and friends' sort. Well connected. Right schools. All the social graces. Rich!' Her tone told him she wasn't any of these—and didn't wish to be.

'Well, if that's my sort, too,' he threw back at her, 'then would you like to explain what I was doing with you?'

Riona had no difficulty answering that one. She'd worked it out on her own a while ago. 'The truth? We both know it. Basically, Cameron, you were slumming it.'

His face went into even tighter lines, but he didn't deny it. Instead he pointed out, 'If you think that, you don't have too high an opinion of yourself either.'

'On the contrary,' she retorted, her voice haughty as she could make it, 'I think myself and my people better than you and yours. We just don't need to dress up and have flash cars and throw big parties to prove it.'

'You just have to be as proud as the devil, is that it?' Cameron suggested in ironical tones, but some of his annoyance seemed to have faded.

'I'm not proud,' Riona claimed, sounding every inch of it.

'Yeah,' Cameron agreed, 'and Reagan wasn't President.'

Riona opened her mouth to argue back, but found no response. He had the last word, and his own way, as the car stopped and, not waiting for Stevens to open their door, he literally pulled her out of the back seat.

'Three hours, back here,' he instructed Stevens briefly, then, keeping tight hold of Riona's hand, walked away from the gardens towards a street lined with shops.

'What about Rory?' she protested, almost tripping to keep up with him.

'Rory will be fine,' he dismissed. 'I didn't just pick Gloria at random. She hopes to train as a nanny, and I think you can be sure she knows the basics. You've been with her all morning. Have you any reason to think differently?' he challenged mid-stride.

Riona had to shake her head. Not only was she a nice girl, but Gloria had proved herself kind and competent in her handling of Rory.

'Right, let's go, because I have to get back to the office some time,' he informed her, before marching her up to the first of several boutiques on Newbury Street. The shop front screamed exclusiveness, the window containing three lifelike dummies draped in silks and chiffons, dresses she couldn't imagine herself wearing in a thousand years.

Cameron, however, pulled her inside and, when an assistant materialised to offer her help, he asked if she could select any day and evening dresses that might suit his companion. It seemed Riona wasn't going to be allowed to choose for herself.

The sales assistant politely looked her up and down and asked her size.

No sooner had she said, 'Twelve', when Cameron contradicted her with, 'Ten. US sizes are different.'

'Oh.' Riona wondered how he knew this. He seemed so at home in the dress shop that it suggested this wasn't his first experience of buying clothes for a woman.

The assistant, at any rate, decided Cameron was the customer and proceeded to consult him exclusively. When she pulled out a selection of dresses and complementary underwear, he was the one to say, 'Yes. No. No. Yes. Yes.'

All Riona had to do was try them on. She resented it at first, but vanity finally got the better of her. How could it not, when she looked in the mirror and saw not a girl but a woman in a black silk slip dress that made her pleased for the first time that she had a figure that curved in all the right places? And wasn't it only natural to wonder if she could rival the beautiful Melissa in a dress like this?

She walked out of the changing-room. Suddenly shy, she didn't look in Cameron's direction. The assistant led her over to a full-sized mirror and Riona stared at her reflection once more, only now doubts crept in about her appearance, especially when there was no comment from Cameron.

It was the assistant who assured her, 'This dress is stunning on you, miss, simply stunning. Don't you think so, sir? She could be a young Kathleen Turner.'

Even Riona knew Kathleen Turner was an American actress, although she wasn't quite sure what she looked like. At any rate, Cameron seemed in no hurry to agree with the assistant.

He came to stand behind Riona and she saw his reflection in the mirror. His eyes ran over the dress before meeting hers in the glass. They stared hard at each other for a moment while the assistant discreetly disappeared into the background. Riona shivered, not because of the dress, but because of the coldness she read in his gaze.

'She's right,' he finally said. 'The dress transforms you. From country girl to sophisticated beauty in one easy move,' he added with a thin smile.

Riona did not smile back. She did not feel complimented.

'If you don't like it,' she answered flatly, 'don't buy it.'

'On the contrary——' his eyes ran down her length once more '—most men would desire you in such a dress and admire me for being the one who possesses you.'

He spoke quietly into her ear, mindful of the assistant. Riona managed, just, to keep her voice down as she hissed back, 'You don't possess me.'

'I know that,' he said, even as he laid a possessive hand on her waist, 'but other men don't. They'll think I'm lucky marrying so beautiful a girl.'

'And you? What do you think?' Riona asked, her heart missing a beat as his fingers spread towards her abdomen.

His eyes caught hers in the mirror again. 'Once I would have thought myself the luckiest man alive.'

Last summer, he meant, and for a brief moment Riona felt herself spun back in time. How he had seemed to love her then. And how she'd loved him. If only...

He pulled her back against him and she did not resist. Voices in the background faded. Everything faded but Cameron. She wanted to turn in his arms, to tell him there was still a chance.

Only he destroyed it as he muttered, 'That was before I wised up, of course,' then pushed her away from him.

She shut her eyes. He'd just been playing with her, trying to hurt her, succeeding.

'We'll take it,' he informed the assistant, and, when Riona walked back towards the changing-room, suggested coldly, 'Try the green one next.'

Later Riona wished she'd rebelled; at the time she'd felt too defeated. She'd put on the clothes he'd suggested and allowed him to decide which to buy. She didn't care. She'd lost all pleasure in her new appearance. Fine clothes hadn't altered his low opinion of her.

She followed him from shop to shop, let him make his selection, and said nothing when he either accepted or rejected what she was wearing.

It took them a mere three hours to purchase three evening dresses, appropriate underwear, six smart daytime outfits that might also be worn at dinner, a collection of heeled shoes in various colours, and some more casual clothes—silk shirts and trousers, and sweat-shirts and jeans, but with designer labels. No mention was made of cost. He simply arranged for any alterations required, signed for them, and requested delivery when they acquired too much to carry home.

'You'll need more,' Cameron announced as they walked back down Newbury Street. 'I'll try to take some time off at the end of the week.'

Riona shook her head. 'No, it's all right. You've bought me enough. It's not as if I'll be in Boston that long.'

'No,' he agreed shortly, 'but, when you return to Invergair, people will expect you to dress up to your new role there.'

Riona made a slight face. She equated 'dressing up' to putting on airs, and she knew that would make her less than popular with her old neighbours. They'd not forget she was once just old Roddy Macleod's grand-daughter—and, if she had any sense, neither would she.

But she didn't argue with him. Her mind was on Rory now. They approached the car to find him once again dozing in the back seat, and she released the breath she'd been subconsciously holding from the moment she'd left him.

They drove back to Harcourt Adams, where Cameron got out of the car; it was already past five in the afternoon, but it seemed he intended to return to work. He left her with a brief, 'See you at dinner. Perhaps you could wear one of your new outfits.'

The suggestion was polite enough but Riona's face went into lines of resentment. He had bought all these

clothes for her so she'd be presentable to his family and
friends. She felt like a doll he was dressing up, only to
ultimately discard.

Yet she seemed to have lost all her backbone as later
she settled Rory for the night, then put on a white silk
blouse and black skirt from her new wardrobe. Both
were beautifully cut, and, with her hair drawn back into
a French plait and her face carefully made up, she
achieved a surprising sophistication. She looked in the
mirror and saw a different girl, someone she didn't know.
She felt less confident than ever when she went down to
dinner.

Cameron wasn't there, just his father, stepmother and
the dreaded Melissa. They all stared as she walked into
the lounge, and she felt as if she'd stepped into enemy
territory. She wanted to flee back upstairs and might have
done so had Cameron's father not stood up to greet her
with a warm, 'Riona, come in. Let's have a look at you...
You look absolutely beautiful,' he declared, smiling
widely as he admired her in her new clothes.

'Thank you,' Riona murmured shyly, not taking the
compliment too seriously. Charles Adams was a nice
man; he saw her lack of confidence and wanted to make
her feel better about herself.

Riona thought the women's reactions were probably
closer to the truth. Melissa Adams, dressed in a dark
red silk dress that made her look exotic, surveyed her
for a moment, then pouted her mouth in dismissal of
the simple outfit. Even in expensive clothes, she was obviously still a nonentity to Melissa. As for Barbara
Adams, she just raised an eyebrow but said nothing.

In fact, the older woman said very little to Riona
throughout dinner. While Charles Adams did his best
to include their guest in conversation, his wife just
stopped short of treating her as invisible. It was rude,
but preferable to Melissa's snide remarks and attempts
to make Riona seem simple.

They were just starting the second course when Cameron materialised. Riona felt relieved at the sight of a familiar if scarcely friendly face. He sat at her side, where a place had already been set.

'Sorry I'm late. I was attempting to clear my desk,' he explained generally.

'Not to worry, son. I'm sure Riona understands.' Charles Adams clearly thought the apology was directed at her.

Riona smiled weakly, reluctant to play the devoted fiancée.

Melissa, however, wasn't going to let her off so easily. 'Do you? I wouldn't have thought so.'

'Melissa.' Cameron raised a warning brow in her direction.

Melissa ignored it. 'I mean, how can she understand? I wouldn't have thought there were too many multi-million-pound corporations among the peat bogs and heather. Correct me if I'm wrong,' she addressed Riona in a cloyingly sweet tone.

'Not many, no,' Riona confirmed shortly.

'And presumably Cameron is the first high-powered executive you've—er—dated—if that isn't a silly word in the—um—circumstances,' Melissa drawled on.

'A very silly word.' Cameron put in before Riona could think of a response. 'So, Mel, if there's a point to this, could we get to it? Then perhaps the rest of us could enjoy our dinner.'

'Sourpuss.' Melissa pulled a playful face at him. 'You don't have to get so uptight. I was actually sympathising with the poor girl.'

She could have fooled Riona.

And Cameron, it seemed, as he echoed, 'You were?'

'Well, it must be hard for her——' she sent Riona a pitying glance '—coming to terms with a completely new environment as well as the expectations you have of her as an executive wife.'

'I have no expectations,' Cameron claimed flatly.

Riona knew he was telling the literal truth. He had no plans for her to fit into his life, long-term.

His father, however, misunderstood, saying, 'Quite right, son. I can't think of anything worse than turning a lovely girl like Riona into a social-climbing executive wife.'

'But perhaps she'd like to be turned,' Melissa persisted, her calculating gaze on Riona. 'She's already started to dress the part. Out of interest, is that outfit Cam's choice or yours?'

'Cameron's,' admitted Riona, gritting her teeth.

'I thought so.' Melissa looked pleased with herself, adding to Cameron, 'I must compliment you on your choice. Simple cut, basic colours—much more flattering for the—shall we say—fuller figure.'

'You can say what you like, Mel.' Cameron actually laughed off the insult—after all, it wasn't directed at him. 'You won't bother Riona. She's too sensible to consider emaciation a fashion statement.'

Riona frowned, neither liking his 'sensible' nor Melissa's comment. In fact, she was getting very tired of being the subject of discussion.

'Garbage,' Melissa continued inelegantly. 'All women long to be thin, just some of us are luckier than others... Perhaps if you ate a little less,' she directed at Riona just as she turned her attention back to her dinner.

For a second or two Riona was too stunned by the other's rudeness to react, then she carefully put down her fork and knife, said with leaden restraint, 'Good idea,' and rose from the table before anyone realised her intention.

Cameron called after her, 'Riona?' but she kept walking, across the dining-room and out into the hall beyond. She would have kept walking if Cameron hadn't caught her on the stairs.

'What are you doing?' He grabbed her arm and wheeled her round.

'What does it look like?' she retorted with all the anger she'd been suppressing. 'I'm going to my room. That way it'll make it even easier for your family to talk as if I'm not there—because I won't be.'

'What? You're not making sense.' He was calm in the face of her temper.

'Aren't I?' she threw back. 'Well, maybe I'm not quite so sensible as you think. Maybe I even mind being called fat!'

'Fat? No one called you fat,' he tried to pacify her.

'Oh, yes, go on. Take her side,' she went on erratically. 'Just don't take me for a fool as well.'

'I don't. I never have,' he declared seriously, 'and I'm not taking Melissa's side. I realise she can be a bitch sometimes. If you want me to have a word with her——'

'And let her think I can't cope,' Riona cut in angrily. 'No, thank you!'

'Then what do you want?' he asked, with heavy patience.

'A one-way ticket back to Scotland,' she answered wildly, but found she meant it, too. These weren't her people. Cameron was no longer her man.

He looked shocked, as if he hadn't expected such a response, but he should have. 'Forget it. We have an agreement. Six months minimum,' he reminded, his hand closing tighter on her arm.

'An agreement?' Riona scoffed at the term. 'Do you really see it like that? You point out how little I have to offer Rory, then you say you'll give him Invergair. And if I don't agree, well, you'll drag us both through a court battle. What choice did I have?'

'What choice did you want?' he snarled back at her. 'Fergus Ross, I suppose. A sailor gone half the year, you scratching a living on Braeside, a baby in your belly after every leave. Is that it?'

Of course, it wasn't, but Riona found herself shouting back, 'Yes, that's it. Why not?'

'You bitch...' He climbed on the step beside her and she struggled to free herself from his grip.

'Let me go!' she spat at him. 'Let me go or I'll scream.'

'Scream away,' he invited, not caring who heard, and lifted a hand to the back of her head.

'Don't...' she breathed in fury, but it was already too late as he brought his mouth down on hers.

He kissed her hard, wanting to hurt, needing to, forcing her to accept, to open her lips to his. She gasped in anger and shock, and he thrust his tongue into the warm recesses of her mouth. She pushed at his chest and tried to twist from the grip of his hand, but he was too strong. He trapped her against the banister and went on kissing her, punishing her for preferring another man, branding her as his.

And all the time Riona's mind cried out in protest, desire flicked through her body like fire. She went on fighting against it, against him, against his terrible power over her, until finally he broke off and pushed her away from him.

He stood for a moment, looking from her bruised mouth to her wild eyes, then cursed with soft violence, 'Damn you. What are you doing to me?'

Riona shook her head. She was doing nothing. He was the one. Destroying.

She shook her head again and he lifted a hand as if to touch her. 'Ree——'

'No!' She backed from him and turned to run.

'Ree...' he called after her, and she was crippled by it, but she kept running.

Why did he call her Ree? Why, when he'd just kissed her as if he hated her? Why, when he'd already killed the girl called Ree, the one he'd loved?

She ran until she reached her room, then she threw herself down on the bed to cry once more for the man she'd loved—gone from her forever.

CHAPTER EIGHT

IT WAS the following evening before Riona saw Cameron again. He appeared in the nursery quarters just as she was finishing bathing the baby.

'I came to see Rory.' He barely glanced at her before fixing his eyes on their son.

'Yes, OK.' She lifted the baby from the bath and wrapped him in a large, fleecy towel.

Cameron sat on a chair while she dressed Rory in his night clothes, then he broke the silence by asking, 'Can I hold him?'

His tone was polite, but it still disconcerted Riona. Last night he'd been almost snarling at her. Now he was being so reasonable. She didn't trust the change.

But she handed over the baby and watched father and son together. Physically they were so alike it hurt. A strong baby, Rory clutched at Cameron's lapels and pulled himself up to half stand on his knee. Cameron took his small hands and helped him bear his weight, and Rory smiled his two-teeth smile before plopping back down.

The game went on for a little while before Rory became tired and anxious and looked round for his mother. Cameron understood and handed him back immediately.

'He'll never really know me.' He spoke his thoughts aloud, and Riona found herself feeling an emotion curiously like guilt.

'I...of course he will,' she answered with a certain optimism. 'He already recognises your face and voice. And when he's older and comes to Boston for his holidays, you'll get to know each other then.'

Cameron looked sceptical. 'I doubt it. By then we'll be polite strangers, nothing more.'

'But I'll tell him about you,' Riona promised, suddenly realising her own selfishness in keeping father and son apart.

'You'll tell him about me,' Cameron echoed, and gave a short hollow laugh. 'And what exactly will you tell him, Riona? That I'm the bastard who ruined your life?'

Riona stared at him in disbelief. Did he really imagine she would be so vindictive? 'You don't think much of me, do you?'

'It's the way you see it, isn't it?' He raised a questioning brow.

Riona didn't know what he wanted her to say. 'Please, Cameron,' she sighed, 'let's not go through it all again. I can't take another fight.'

There was real weariness in her voice. She'd been woken twice in the night by Rory, and had spent a long day in the nursery, brooding. She held Rory to her now, her face shadowed by unhappiness.

Though she'd admitted her vulnerability, the last thing she expected was Cameron to relent. Yet he did, saying, 'I'm sorry. Believe it or not, I didn't mean things to go like this.' He shoved his hands into his pockets and walked towards the window, before adding, 'I promised myself I'd be calm and rational but, round you, things never seem to work out that way.'

Riona understood well enough. It was the same for her. Every time he walked into a room, her body tensed and her thoughts became a jumble.

'Look, I'd like to visit Rory every evening. If we could call a truce...' He faced her once more.

'I...' She hesitated, not really believing a truce was possible between them.

'I don't think either of us could take another six months' fighting,' he added, his tone revealing some of the strain he was under, too.

Riona looked at him properly for the first time. He was dressed in a dark conservative suit and white shirt. The silk tie at his neck had been pulled down and the top button opened. He looked grey and drained, very different from the man he'd been in Invergair.

'All right,' Riona murmured in vague agreement, then indicated Rory growing restless in her arms. 'I have to give him his last feed.'

'Yes, OK.' Cameron recognised it as a dismissal and, for once, accepted it. 'I'll see you at dinner,' he told her, and, lightly touching his son's head in farewell, left before she could contradict him.

After last night Riona would happily have dined in her room. But she was no coward and, with Rory tucked up for the night, she changed into a green silk blouse and elegant black trousers. Then she reluctantly went down to dinner.

She wondered what to expect from Melissa, but, apart from flicking her a hostile glance on entrance, the American girl proceeded to ignore her throughout the meal.

So did Barbara Adams, but Riona was growing used to that. She was a chilly, distant woman whose conversation with her husband was limited to household requirements and social events. Had there been any love between her and Cameron's father, it seemed to have long since died. They treated each other like polite acquaintances, no more.

Riona recognised this because it mirrored the way Cameron treated her. Not that the family seemed to notice the lack of any real warmth between them. Perhaps it was normal for upper-class Bostonians to behave with such cool reserve, but Riona found herself longing for the Cameron who had been wild and funny and so alive.

Melissa, however, wasn't put off by this more aloof Cameron as she did her best to monopolise his attention with questions about the business and remarks about mutual friends and some pretty blatant flirting.

'You mustn't mind Melissa,' Charles Adams said later as they drank coffee in the lounge while Cameron went outside to look over a new sports car the other girl had purchased and Barbara Adams disappeared altogether. 'She's always looked up to Cameron, doted on him as a big brother. I guess she's a little jealous now he's finally getting married.'

'It's all right.' Riona wondered if the older man could be really that naïve about Melissa's interest in Cameron, but she saw no point in disagreeing with him. After all, *she* wasn't jealous. Was she?

'Well, I just don't want you to get any wrong ideas,' Charles ran on. 'Speaking for myself, I'm more than delighted that you're marrying Cameron, and, while you're living in this house, I want you to feel at home.'

'Thank you.' Riona smiled, grateful for his kindness.

'You know we have some tennis courts out back,' he volunteered. 'I'm sure Melissa would give you a game.'

It was an unwelcome idea and Riona was relieved she could say, 'I'm afraid I don't play. I'm not very sporty.'

'Never mind,' Charles dismissed his suggestion, adding, 'What sort of thing do you like doing, then?'

'At home?' Riona thought for a moment before admitting, 'Nothing very exciting. I read a little, play the piano, go for walks.'

'You play piano,' her future father-in-law echoed with interest. 'Well, that's one thing you could do here. There's a piano in the music-room—rather a fine one. How well do you play?'

'Competently enough,' Riona said with some modesty, before explaining, 'My grandfather taught me. He was brilliant. With formal training, he could have been concert standard.'

'What about you?' Charles asked. 'Did you ever have any formal training?'

She shook her head. 'I was actually lucky enough to win a place at the Royal College in Edinburgh, but I never got round to taking it up. I suppose I'm not really dedicated enough.'

'Or maybe you had your eye on greater things?' was suggested in sarcastic tones, not by Charles Adams, but by Melissa, who returned through the French windows that opened out on to the terrace at the rear of the house. 'Imagine, a potential Stravinsky in our midst, and you gave it up for poor old Cameron... Well, maybe not quite so poor.'

'Shut up, Melissa,' came from Cameron, who was standing by her side, but there was little force in his words.

Instead it was against Riona his anger seemed directed, as he stared hard at her. His dark blue eyes seemed to accuse her of something, but what was the question?

'Come on, Melissa.' Charles Adams stood up and took his stepdaughter's arm. 'Let's go play some billiards. You can take things out on me.'

Riona had thought the older man an amiable character without his son's force of personality, but he proved otherwise as he marched a protesting Melissa out of the room.

The moment they were alone, Cameron demanded, 'Why didn't you tell me you had a college place?'

Riona shrugged in response. 'It didn't seem important. I wasn't able to take it up, anyway.'

'Yeah, and why was that?' Cameron's tone was sceptical, as if he expected some poor excuse for her lack of ambition, but then he suddenly worked out the answer for himself. 'You had to look after your grandfather instead.'

'I didn't *have* to,' Riona stressed, 'I wanted to. I suppose you could say if I'd been really talented or ambitious I would have chosen college.'

Riona had admitted as much to herself some time ago. Dedicated musicians let little or nothing in the way of their music. She wasn't like that. She wasn't single-minded enough and she didn't rate music above everything else.

'You did what you considered right at the time.' Cameron seemed to agree with her decision. 'But why didn't you go to college later?'

'Last September, you mean...?' Riona trailed off, feeling he could answer that one for himself, too.

In actual fact, she had reapplied to the music school at the beginning of the summer, but then she had met Cameron, and all thought of college had flown out of the window. Her acceptance had arrived three weeks after he left, but by then it had meant nothing to her. Nothing had meant anything by that time.

She said none of this—but Cameron saw the pain of memory cross her face. 'I really loused up your life, didn't I?'

Riona could have left him thinking that. After all, didn't he deserve the guilt? Yet her need for truth was stronger than any desire to punish him.

'Don't flatter yourself,' she answered carelessly. 'I could have still gone to college if I'd wanted. I just didn't want it enough.'

'For God's sake, I'm not a fool. You were pregnant with my child.' Cameron suddenly seemed to realise the effect it had had on her life.

But Riona decided he could keep his guilt. It was a poor substitute for the love he had once given her.

She shrugged her shoulders and said dismissively, 'Well, it hardly matters now. I have Rory. Life goes on.'

'You make things sound so simple.' He searched her face for signs of weakness but saw none. 'Can you really forget our past so easily?'

Riona could have told him no. Could have told him how she remembered everything—every word, every glance, every touch of the hand—from their brief love affair. But what would be the point?

'I have to,' she answered in a hard, flat voice, and, before he could pursue it, walked past him to the door.

She half expected him to call her back, but he simply followed her out into the hall and watched her as she climbed the stairs to her room.

She didn't cry that night but she lay in bed, sleepless, trying to understand him. She still did not know what he wanted from her. All along she had made it easy for him: she hadn't asked for his help when pregnant; she accepted it now without argument or recriminations. Yet he seemed to need to make things as painful as possible. Did Cameron really hate her so much?

She decided he must and was on her guard the next evening when he came to see Rory, but he said nothing controversial. He played with the baby a little, then departed. They saw each other at dinner and it was a rerun of the previous night. Melissa dominated the conversation, excluding Riona with talk of people she didn't know.

Riona didn't object. It seemed pointless to fight for a place in a family where she didn't belong. In fact, it wasn't Melissa's hostility or Barbara's coldness that made her feel bad, but Charles Adams's enthusiasm for the marriage.

It was Charles who talked wedding plans, asking whether they intended a civil or church ceremony. Cameron deferred to her, and she chose civil as the least hypocritical in the circumstances. Charles then pressed Cameron about what sort of house they planned on buying. Cameron surprised her by claiming they'd decided on a townhouse in the city. She only just stopped her jaw from dropping open, and, while Charles discussed the pros and cons of such a choice, she marvelled at the ease with which Cameron lied.

Later, when his father again insisted on them having time alone, she felt she had to say something. 'Cameron, I realise your father put you on the spot, but did you have to make up that about a townhouse?'

'I didn't,' Cameron replied succinctly.

'You didn't what?'

'Make it up... I thought we could look for a house this weekend.'

This time Riona's jaw did drop open. 'To buy, you mean?'

'Or rent. Whichever's going to give us the quickest entry date,' he explained.

'But... you want to leave here?' Riona had taken for granted that they would remain in his father's house rather than set up a temporary home elsewhere.

'I assumed *you'd* want to.' He raised a questioning brow. 'It can't be easy for you living in someone else's house, especially my stepmother's. After all, she doesn't even make my father feel welcome,' he added drily.

'I...' Riona didn't know how to respond. The thought of her own house, where she didn't have to creep around avoiding Barbara and Melissa, was very tempting. But the thought of her and Cameron alone, without any restraint on their tempers, was less exciting.

'Don't worry.' He misread her expression. 'We're talking a strictly impersonal set-up. A bedroom each.'

'I didn't mean that,' she denied. 'I was just wondering whether we could live in—er—harmony.'

'Probably not,' Cameron conceded with a wry twist, 'but we could at least try. And you won't see much of me, considering my work hours.'

'But won't it be an expense——' Riona felt uncomfortable with his generosity '—buying a house just for six months?'

He shook his head. 'I'll need a bigger place anyway, when Rory comes to visit... So what do you think?'

Riona decided to be honest. 'I think it's a wonderful idea.'

'OK, we'll go house-hunting this weekend.' He smiled at her enthusiasm.

Riona smiled back, imagining for a moment they were really starting a new life together.

She remained in buoyant mood for the rest of the week, until the Friday evening, when Melissa heard about their proposed move and, waiting till they were alone, reminded Riona that her hold on Cameron was only temporary.

Riona was never sure what to believe of Melissa's claims. She maintained she was Cameron's real choice and only Rory was obliging him to marry elsewhere. Yet Riona had seen no evidence to support this. Melissa might flirt with Cameron, but he seemed to laugh most of it off.

Melissa's nastiness, however, still lingered the next day, as Riona drove into Boston with Cameron, Rory strapped in a baby-chair in the back.

'I've selected five houses to view, all near the park,' he relayed, handing her over some real-estate papers. When she didn't comment, he added, 'I assumed you'd prefer a house, but we could look at some apartments instead.'

'No, a house would be fine,' Riona responded flatly.

'Look, if you've gone off the idea...' He glanced from the road to her, trying to gauge her mood.

'It's not that. It's just...' Just your stepsister. She could hardly say that. At least, she could. She could ask him straight out if Melissa was right—if, freed from obligations, he'd sooner marry the American girl. But did she really want to know the answer?

'It's nothing. I was just wondering what we'd do for furniture,' she said off the top of her head.

'No problem,' he dismissed. 'I've arranged credit facilities for you. If we find a suitable house, you can buy furniture next week and arrange delivery for our entry date.'

'I'm not sure that's such a good idea. I've never furnished a house before.' Riona doubted her taste would please him.

He shrugged. 'Get what you like. It's your house.'

Her house. If only it was, Riona thought as she imagined for a moment this whole thing was real—that they were still in love, and marrying was a joy, and their first house together was an adventure. But none of that was true.

She let herself pretend a little, however, as they met the estate agent and went round a variety of houses, comparing one with the other. They all seemed beautiful—not massive and intimidating like his father's, but still large, with well-proportioned rooms, decorated in such style; she couldn't help thinking of the contrast between them and her small, dark crofthouse.

In the end, she left Cameron to make the choice. He picked a three-storey brownstone close to the park which was already vacant and available for almost immediate possession. In a fortnight they might be ready to move.

As suggested, Riona went furniture shopping the following week. She insisted on travelling by train rather than having Stevens trail after her. She took Gloria, however, to help with Rory, and daily they visited the shops. Riona enjoyed it, as she formed a picture of their living-room, bedrooms and kitchen, but she never let herself lose sight of reality. Mentally she chose every stick of furniture for the house but *bought* none of it.

It was a dream, and she knew it. Even as Cameron and she suddenly began to talk again, and plan, and laugh a little, she knew it wasn't going to last. Something would spoil the dream and force her to wake up.

The something happened on the Friday evening. Cameron's father had decided to give a dinner party so friends could meet his son's future bride. Riona dreaded the event and was surprised when Melissa seemed to look forward to it, but eventually a few sly hints from the other girl told her why. Faced with the sophistication of their guests, Melissa had high hopes Riona would prove a social disaster.

Melissa was very possibly right, Riona thought, as she walked down the wide marble staircase for dinner, but she still held her head up and tried to conceal her nerves.

Cameron was waiting for her at the foot of the stairs. He stared up at her without smiling. She wondered if she'd dressed wrongly. She was wearing the black silk slip dress for the first time, with her hair arranged in a chignon by a surprisingly expert Gloria. The other girl declared her the last word in elegance and Riona, too, had been pleased with her image in the bedroom mirror. Now she began to have second thoughts as a frown creased Cameron's forehead.

She expected no compliments by the time she reached his side and was surprised when he said, 'I've never seen you look so beautiful.'

'Thank you,' she responded softly and trembled a little as his hand closed over hers.

'Nervous?' he asked as he led her towards the living-room, where the guests were gathered for pre-dinner drinks.

'Petrified,' she admitted frankly.

'You don't have to be,' he assured her. 'None of them is really important.'

To her, she supposed he meant. After all, did it matter if she made a fool of herself? She was never going to be part of his world.

She didn't really want to be, Riona decided, too, as she sat through an interminably long dinner party. She had little in common with women who talked of clothes and health clinics and exercise plans, their whole lives dedicated to remaining young and beautiful-looking. And the men, they talked of business deals, and proposed mergers, and making money, as if it were a religion.

Knowing nothing of such things, Riona didn't contribute much to the conversation. Not that she was expected to. She forced a smile when the men complimented her or Cameron on her beauty, and lost pleasure in her appearance as they treated her like an acquisition. The women were no better, coming mostly from the Barbara Adams school of chilly charm.

Melissa held court over the younger guests. Riona could hear her raised voice from the far end of the table, and, when she glanced downwards, she met two or three pairs of curious eyes. She was probably being paranoid, but she felt herself to be the cause of the mocking laughter that followed.

It wasn't really a surprise later when she had her suspicions confirmed. It was after dinner when the guests had drifted back through to the lounge. As it was a warm night, the French windows had been thrown open and the younger, noisier crowd gathered outside on the terrace, their spirits lifted further by the drink being liberally supplied by two floating waiters.

Although they might also have been his friends, Cameron seemed to deliberately stay clear of this crowd, and, keeping Riona at his side, ensured she stayed clear, too.

Riona didn't object as she began to relax in the company of a couple called the Van Sykeses, whom Cameron introduced as close friends. Blair, the woman, seemed different from the rest, talking more of her young family than what beauty treatments she favoured, and, displaying no embarrassment, asked Riona straight out about Rory. Very soon they were swapping baby stories and Riona forgot to be nervous.

The woman was just suggesting a lunch date when Charles Adams approached, and, politely excusing himself, took Cameron to one side. Cameron frowned at whatever his father had to say, then excused himself and headed outside to the terrace.

Riona didn't understand what was going on, but possibly the Van Sykeses did as they both broke into conversation at the same time in an obvious attempt to distract her.

They could not drown out Melissa, however, as she came in from the terrace, her over-loud voice drawing curious eyes.

Cameron was at her side. In fact, he had hold of her wrist, with the intention of heading for the door, but Melissa, obviously more than a little drunk, resisted, and dug her heels in when they came near to Riona.

'How do you love him? I've bet you've counted the ways,' she burst out in a shrill parody of song, then laughed as Cameron forced her on.

He threw Riona an apologetic look, but it didn't make up for the embarrassment. The Van Sykeses smiled kindly, too, but Riona's face remained frozen as she tried to hide her feelings.

Worse was to come as raised voices drifted in from the terrace.

'Clever old Melissa,' a female voice applauded. 'She said she'd get him and she has.'

'It looked more the other way round,' her male companion remarked on Cameron's summary treatment of a drunken Melissa.

'Don't kid yourself. She's managed to prise him away from Little Miss Nonentity, hasn't she?' the woman crowed, to be greeted by general laughter.

Riona stood where she was and listened. She could hear Blair Van Sykes desperately trying to distract her with conversation, but none of it penetrated.

'So who wants to take a bet on the result?' a new voice chimed in.

'Well, I'll give you ten to one he marries Melissa in the end,' the woman threw back.

'You think so?' A male voice cast doubt on it. 'Nonentity she may be, but I certainly wouldn't kick her out of bed on a cold morning.'

It was a compliment of sorts, but Riona felt defiled by it. Still she kept listening. She had needed these clever, sarcastic, sickening people to wake her up to reality:

'Look, ignore it.' Blair tried to draw her away. 'They're just drunk and being stupid. You mustn't...' She broke off, as she realised Riona wasn't listening to her.

The loud woman was speaking again. 'Come on, guys, get real. A pretty face with bastard in tow, against brains, beauty and a major stockholding in HA. No contest.'

No contest. The words echoed in Riona's head as she finally walked away from the scene and made her way through the crowd. The Van Sykeses called her back but she kept walking until she was out in the chequered hall. She meant to keep walking until she was in her room, but she heard other voices—Melissa's alternatively pleading and teasing, Cameron's too gruff and low to catch. They came from the music-room.

Go on upstairs, her own inner voice told her, but she was compelled to listen to the others.

The door was open. The scene didn't need any explanation. Melissa had both arms round Cameron's neck, her body pressed to his. He wasn't protesting. It was a surprise that they even noticed her—the nonentity standing in the doorway.

'Riona.' Cameron frowned at seeing her there, and, when she turned, he called out, 'Riona, wait!'

This time Riona didn't walk. She ran. She ran until she reached the safety of her own room.

She sought privacy to break down, but had forgotten Gloria was still there, listening out for Rory in case he waked. She managed to control her emotions and thank Gloria, before ushering her out of the room.

Even then she didn't get a chance to sort out her feelings, as Cameron walked into the room without knocking. He closed the door behind him and leaned against the frame, blocking her exit.

'Get out of my room!' Riona whispered fiercely at him, unable to scream with Rory next door.

He ignored her. 'We have to talk. I assume from your hurried departure you've jumped to a reasonable but quite wrong conclusion.'

He selected his words carefully. He was so calm that Riona wanted to spit.

'Oh, really,' she threw back at him, 'and what conclusion could I possibly have drawn from Melissa climbing all over you...? Don't tell me. You had something in your eye.'

His jaw tightened at her sarcasm. 'Look, I didn't have to come up here. I don't *have* to explain anything to you, either.'

'Good! Then don't!' Riona didn't want him to lie to her. She just wanted him to leave.

But he seemed in no hurry to go. 'Do you know, Ree, if I didn't know better, I'd say you were jealous.'

'*Jealous*?' Riona virtually exploded. 'Don't flatter yourself. If you want Melissa, you have her, and may you both live happily ever after,' she said, attempting indifference, but making it sound more like a curse.

'Oh, that would suit you, wouldn't it?' He pushed away from the door and came towards her. 'I jilt you for Melissa, but still hand over Invergair to Rory... Well, forget it. We get married as planned.'

'This is absurd!' Riona turned away from him and crossed to the window. She looked down to the courtyard and saw the first guests leaving. 'Neither of us wants it, so who are we marrying for? The rest of the world? The rest of the world is downstairs and they think you're crazy for marrying an nonentity like me. In fact, they probably agree with Melissa—that I'm after your money,' she added, turning to face him once more.

He seemed unmoved. 'So? It's what *I* think that counts?'

'And what *do* you think?' Riona suspected he too saw her as a gold-digger, but he avoided a direct answer.

'We marry as agreed,' he said instead. 'I've already made the arrangements. The ceremony is in three weeks at City Hall. We need blood tests first, however.'

His tone was flat and factual, as if they were talking of a dental appointment or a visit to the doctor—something that was unpleasant but had to be faced.

She shook her head. 'I won't marry you, Cameron. I can't. Not even for Invergair.' She appealed for him to recognise what they were doing to each other. 'It isn't right, Cameron. Don't you see?'

'Right?' He growled the word at her, his indifference suddenly changed to anger, and, when she would have backed away from him, he grabbed at her arms. 'Since when have you worried about what's right? You sleep with me. You sleep with your sailor boy. Then you have a baby, not knowing or caring whose it is. Yet suddenly you're an authority on what's right.'

'It wasn't like that!' Riona struggled hopelessly to free herself. 'I knew whose baby he was. I knew from the beginning. I just wanted——'

'Rory to be his,' he concluded wildly. 'I know that. Do you think I don't? But he's my son, just as you're going to be my wife. And Fergus Ross will never have you again.'

'Cameron!' She stared up at him, hearing the bitter passion in his voice, and saw it reflected in his eyes. 'You're all wrong. I——'

She began to reason with him, but he cut across her. 'I'd kill you first, Ree. Do you understand? I'd kill you.' His hands tightened on her arms, telling her he meant every word.

'I—I...' Riona tried to find a response, but her mouth went dry. She felt her heart beating dangerously fast, and told herself it was fear of his jealousy.

But she really knew better. She wasn't an innocent young girl any more. She recognised his arousal just as she recognised her own. She felt physical desire as sharp as any pain and knew he felt the same. He didn't want to kill her, he wanted...

'No.' She breathed the word and tried to back away from him.

'Yes.' His fingers relaxed their hurting hold, but he wouldn't let her go. 'This is what's right, Ree. The rest means nothing.'

Riona shut her eyes so she couldn't see his face, couldn't mistake the sudden intensity of desire for love. It couldn't be right that he should want her like this, even as he hated her with every word he'd uttered. He touched her cheek and she trembled. He pressed his lips to her brow with all the old tenderness and all the old longing came back in a wave. 'Just once more.' He spoke with the urgency of need. 'I have to, Ree... Just once more...'

She could have pretended not to understand. She could have pretended not to feel the same way. But she couldn't help herself. Though she pleaded, 'Don't do this to me, Cam,' she made no move to avoid the mouth seeking hers.

She knew it was the road to more pain, yet she had to walk down it. The moment his lips touched hers, her head began to swim, and if she cried in protest, 'Not again,' the words came out as a moan, betraying her. He kissed her, soft and persuasive, then harder, until the rush of desire filled her head and she opened her mouth to him in surrender.

But it wasn't enough. It had never been enough as, still kissing her, he pushed her back against the wall and lifted a hand to the fullness of her breast. His fingers moved over the silk of her dress, remembering, wanting, needing the warm silk of her skin.

He pulled her body to his and, with a rough urgency, dragged down the zip of her dress. She felt it slipping and held the silk to her, ashamed of how easily he could seduce her. He started to kiss her again, his hand in her hair, gently pulling her head back, softly touching his lips to her throat until she was weak with longing for him.

She moaned aloud and sought his mouth with hers, need overcoming shame. He kissed her hard, as if he wanted to leave an imprint on her mouth for ever, but his hands were gentle, sliding over her bare arms, slowly pushing away the thin straps of her dress until the silk fell from her body.

Then he stood back from her, holding her arms so she could not hide herself. The black basque she wore underneath scarcely covered her breasts and was more provocative than if she'd been naked.

'You're so beautiful.' He spoke the words in a whisper and a pain gripped her heart, as she heard echoes of the love he'd once felt for her.

She told herself this was just sex, but it made no difference. When he reached out a hand to slowly unfasten the silk ties of the basque, she stood there, trembling. When he pushed the silk apart, she shut her eyes at the old familiar wanting she felt for him. She kept them shut as he stripped away the basque, his fingers barely brushing her skin.

She was his once more and he knew it. He saw the sensual curve of her mouth, bruised by his kiss, the half-drugged look in her eyes. He said nothing, perhaps fearing words might bring her back to her senses, and, pulling off his tie, began to unbutton his shirt.

She frowned slightly and lifted her arms to cover her breasts. He reached for her again, and turned her round to kiss the soft downy skin at her neck and shoulders. She shivered a little, but did not pull away as his arms encircled her waist, drawing her naked back against his chest.

He held her there, to the warmth of his skin, and she closed her eyes to reality. Cameron was her lover. He would always be her lover. The rest was the dream. How could it be otherwise when they'd been made for each other?

She turned in his arms, or he turned her. It didn't matter. She was willing. She let him look at her and his eyes travelled over the pale translucent skin of her shoulders down to her naked breasts, still full and

beautiful, seemingly untouched by child-bearing. He
stared hard at her, making love to her in his mind, and
the breath caught in her throat. Slowly he unpinned her
hair and let it fall down her back. Then he came closer
again and bowed his head and, before she realised his
intention, took the hard aching peak of her breast in his
mouth.

She cried out, in shock and pain and pleasure, as he
began to play and bite and suck on her yielding flesh,
and Cameron groaned his own need of her, as he recalled the soft, sensual girl with whom he'd once thought
himself in love. He remembered it all—the days and
nights spent together, loving—and past and present fused
so easily. He slipped an arm under her knees and carried
her to the bed. He laid her down and just held her for
a moment.

With a last shred of sanity Riona realised they were
on the point of no return. She saw her future repeating
itself in the same terrible cycle—her love going on and
on, while his loving proved a transitory thing. Did she
want this—one more vivid memory to try and forget?

'No, I can't!' The words came in a breathless rush,
almost inaudible, but he was so close that he must have
heard. He chose not to listen.

Instead he responded to his own compulsion, and, as
his lips fastened on hers, stilled any further cry. Riona
felt herself drowning in the fierce tide of his desire and
tried to save herself. She pushed at his naked shoulders,
curled nailed fingers into his back, but it was no use.
Even as she sought to hurt him, her mouth opened to
his and accepted the thrusting intimacy of his tongue.

He kissed her and touched her and made her want
him in all the ways he knew how, until it was she who
arched to him, who offered her body, her love. It was
she who groaned as his mouth left hers, once more
seeking her breasts, licking and teasing each nipple until
she grasped his dark head and wordlessly begged him to
suck harder her aching flesh.

Cameron pleasured her until he could stand her small, sweet moans of desire no longer, and rose from the bed to strip off the rest of his clothing. All the time he held her eyes, and she held his, imagining she saw love in their warm blue gaze. She always had before. It helped her now to shut out doubts and accept what was happening—what she wanted to happen—without the shame of thinking herself used.

He came to her, and they lay for a moment, side by side, in wonder at being like this again. Then they kissed with a sweetness that seemed to go beyond sex, before desire took over once more. His mouth trailed downwards, touching her throat, her breasts, every curve of her body, before it reached the most intimate part of her and shocked her with this half-forgotten pleasure. She cried aloud again, but he continued to make love to her in this way until she moaned her need and slid down the bed to wrap her body round his.

Cameron felt his own control slipping and, pressing her back down on the bed, lifted himself above her. Their eyes met for a moment, and he savoured it—having her beneath him once more. Then he thrust himself inside her with a passion that was almost anger.

She flinched and, aware of every movement of her body, he went still. 'I hurt you.'

Riona shook her head, but he knew she was lying.

'The baby... our baby... perhaps...' He voiced half-formed ideas of why she might hurt and started to withdraw.

Riona shook her head and held him to her, wanting him more than ever, for the words 'our baby' melted her heart. It was the first time he'd called Rory that. Maybe things could be different, maybe...

The thought trailed off as he moved inside her and this time brought desire rather than pain. She reached out for him, telling him with her body that everything was all right.

She'd never wanted him so much—the heat of him, the smell of him, him inside her, only him. She clutched at him, cried for him, drowned in him, gave herself so completely that he called out his need for her even as his seed spilled inside her.

God, I need you. Need you. Need you... The words echoed inside Riona's head, as she too left reality for dreams, dreamt that this could be reality, Cameron and her together, bound by passion, bound by love, bound for a lifetime, because how could it be otherwise?

It was a beautiful dream. She wanted it to go on for ever, but hearts slowed and bodies cooled, and dreams faded all too easily. Reality was Riona Macleod, a misfit in this sophisticated world. And Cameron Adams—rich, successful, needing her only in one way.

Riona faced it and accepted it and grew proud on the humiliation of it. She forced herself to pull away from the arm still round her and, holding the sheet to her breasts, sat up in the narrow bed.

'You'd better go,' she said almost coldly. 'Someone might be looking for you.'

'So?' He seemed indifferent to his family as he lay where he was and stretched out a lazy hand to touch her back.

She shivered and felt her resolve weakening. Any moment he would reach for her and they'd make love again, and she'd forget once more that she had no real place in his life.

She shook her head, and, before he could draw her back down, said, 'So I'd like you to go. Now. Before anyone discovers us.'

'Does it matter?' he replied, and she could hear the smile in his voice as he came up to sit beside her in the narrow bed. 'We'll be married soon.'

She shrugged off the hand that started to caress her shoulder, and hardened her heart to him. 'It seems you weren't listening earlier. I won't marry you, Cameron.'

'What? You can't mean that.' He reached an arm to switch on the bedside light, then half turned her in the bed to face him.

She lifted her head back a little, a deliberately proud gesture that also unconsciously displayed her beauty, the blonde hair streaming back from her face to reveal wide green eyes and a sulky pout. She knew she was provoking an argument, but that seemed the best way out.

'Why can't I? Did you think a quick...quick roll in the hay——' she deliberately cheapened their love-making '—was going to change things?'

'Why, you...' Cameron broke off and made a grab for her arm, but she was already scrambling off the bed.

He followed and caught her before she could seek sanctuary in Rory's room. He pulled her round and shoved her against the wall. Frightened now, Riona tried to twist out of his grip, but he trapped her body with his. She realised his intention and violently shook her head as she tried to escape the mouth seeking hers, but he grabbed a handful of her hair and forced her head up.

It was a kiss of punishment, wanting to hurt her, needing to hurt her for her cruel, careless words. Then gradually it turned into something else as the heat from his hard, naked body lit a fire in her own. She felt desire kick in her stomach as his lips left hers to travel downwards over the damp silk of her skin. In a moment she would be lost again.

'Don't...' she cried out and pushed hard at his shoulders.

Her rejection was unmistakable and he cursed crudely under his breath. He took a step back from her, and she saw anger and frustration in his face. 'You want me, Ree. You'll always want me. Why fight it?'

'Because it's just sex, Cameron,' she threw back at him, angry too that she'd been so close to letting him use her again. 'Just sex and it means nothing!'

She shouted so loudly the whole house might have heard. He visibly flinched, then looked ready to hit her. He raised a hand and slammed it hard against the wall behind.

Riona felt a moment's fright, then anger, as a wail came from the adjoining room. They had woken Rory.

'He needs me.' She gave him a look of contempt that demanded her release and he let her go.

She covered her nakedness with a bathrobe, and, without another word, went through to her son.

She returned thirty minutes later, and he was gone.

She tried to tell herself she'd won—she'd sent him away. But pride did nothing to take away the ache in her heart.

What a fool she'd been. He'd taken her out of need and she'd let him. She'd let him, because, for a little while, she'd imagined that there might be more, that there *had* to be more—the way he touched her, looked at her, made love to her. She'd refused to see that he was just using her.

But, with passion spent, she'd seen things as they really were. She'd provided temporary relief, nothing more.

And that was the last time. She couldn't let him turn her around again. The pleasure might be acute, but the pain was terminal.

No more, Riona promised herself, no more.

CHAPTER NINE

RIONA left the following day. She didn't plan it. She just did it. She saw Cameron speed away in his car with Melissa in the passenger seat and she knew she couldn't take the pain.

She didn't stop and think of Rory and Invergair. Having barely slept, she was no longer operating on sense or logic.

She threw clothes in one suitcase—the clothes they had arrived with—and simply walked downstairs and out of the door. No one stopped her. No one saw her.

She walked until she reached the station, carrying the case in one hand, pushing Rory's buggy with the other. It was all remarkably simple—a train into Boston, taxi to the airport, flight to New York then on to another for London. By the time she arrived at Heathrow, Rory's sleep pattern was so disrupted that she thought she might just as well carry on. Two trains later, she had caught the old bus for Invergair.

She paid for nearly all of it with the American Express card Cameron had given her. She had no qualms about it. In the end he'd thank her. He'd marry Melissa and have more children and breathe a sigh of relief that she and Rory had disappeared from his life.

She arrived in Invergair on the Sunday evening, almost drunk with exhaustion. She'd been travelling for thirty-six hours.

She walked up from the bus-stop in the drizzling West Coast rain to Dr Macnab's house with a sleeping Rory in her arms. She looked as bone-weary as she felt when the doctor opened the door to her.

If she expected a surprised reaction from the old doctor, she was disappointed. He acted rather as if he would have been surprised had she not returned, Rory in tow, and, to her relief, didn't bombard her with questions.

Instead he sat her down with Rory still asleep in her arms, asked her when she'd last eaten, and disappeared to make sandwiches.

He waited while she ate a little, then asked simply, 'Are you home to stay, lass?'

'Aye, I think so,' she replied, then added simply, 'Nothing was right, Doctor.'

'No,' the old man said with an understanding nod, and didn't press for any further explanation.

Riona remembered just why she liked the doctor so much. 'I've missed you, Doctor.'

'Aye, myself as well, lass.' He confirmed his fondness for her in the same restrained Scottish fashion, before becoming his usual bluff self and insisting she remain at his house overnight.

Riona didn't put up much of a fight. She was too tired to argue, and saw the sense in it when the doctor pointed out that her croft might need some airing.

He used the same argument next day, in persuading her to leave Rory with Mrs Ross, his housekeeper, while he drove her up to Braeside at the start of his rounds and left her to check over the place.

As she walked up the hill, Riona felt her spirits sinking. If anything, the croft looked more dilapidated than ever. In Boston, homesickness had made her remember only the good things about Invergair—the simplicity of the life, the honesty of the people. Her unhappiness had made her forget just how little she had to offer Rory.

She walked with head bowed until she rounded the side of the crofthouse. She half expected Jo to appear; though a neighbour was taking care of him, she knew the collie would wander back here occasionally. But there was no sign of him as she searched for the back-door key under the stone where she always left it. She found it but, when she turned it in the lock, the door remained shut. She turned the key again and the door opened. She assumed she hadn't locked it. No alarm bells rang until she'd entered the kitchen, and by then it was too late.

He was standing quite calmly by the sink, a cup in his hand.

He laid the cup down, saying, 'Hello, Ree.'

For a moment Riona felt she'd gone back in time to last summer. Then he'd had the right to let himself into her home, into her life. Not now.

She started to ask him what he was doing there, but the words dried in her throat. It was obvious why he was here—to take them back to America.

She shook her head. 'I won't go with you.'

'Look, Ree, we have to...' He moved towards her and she panicked.

Her hand on the door, she flung it open and ran blindly. She heard him behind her, calling. 'Come on, Riona, don't be stupid! Let's talk.'

But Riona didn't want to sit down and talk. She didn't want to listen to all the reasons she should go through a pretence of a marriage, all the things he would give their son and all the things she never could.

She continued running up the hill, thrashing her way through the gorse and heather, ignoring his shouts to stop, the sounds of him chasing after her.

He caught her halfway up, grabbing at her jacket. Desperation gave her strength and she tore her arm free, striking out with the other. She hit him hard and, surprised by the attack, he let her go. But her freedom was temporary, as he chased her on up the hill and, no longer making concessions for her sex, brought her down with a leg tackle.

The heather cushioned her fall, but the wind was knocked from her. While she struggled for breath, he dragged her round and held her there.

'You crazy little...' He broke off as she freed an arm and tried to punch him with it. 'Quit that. Quit that or maybe I'll forget you're a woman!'

Riona wasn't impressed by the threat. She knew Cameron too well. He had never physically hurt her and he never would.

She continued to struggle and he straddled her, pinning an arm to each side of her head. Even Riona knew by then that he had her trapped, but panic had turned to anger and she kept trying to buck him off her with her hips until she exhausted herself.

Then she lay underneath him, breathing hard, but not admitting defeat while her eyes could burn with anger.

There was no answering anger on Cameron's face, as he held her, admiring her splendid Celtic temper, and her foolish courage, and her wild, natural beauty. For, far from forgetting she was a woman, the struggling body beneath him made him all too aware of it.

Their eyes met and held, and Riona felt her fury beginning to fade. In its place came the familiar weakness, the first stirring of another passion catching the breath in her throat.

'No.' She shook her head as his mouth descended towards hers, and cried out against it, 'No, Cameron! No!'

She couldn't go through this again. If she let him take her once more, she would have no pride left, and, without pride, how could she carry on?

What stopped him? Not her words, perhaps, but the tears that sparked in her eyes. Or a realisation that they were destroying each other.

Whichever, he suddenly pushed himself away from her, and, standing, reached a hand down to pull her up. Riona swayed a little on her feet, but wasn't given the time to regain her balance as he dragged her along after him.

He kept hold of her hand until they reached the croft and were in the kitchen once more. It was just as well as Riona suddenly felt too tired to stand on her own two feet.

'Sit down. You look terrible,' Cameron said with unflattering directness.

Riona didn't argue, sinking down on one of the old, rickety chairs at the kitchen table. In hindsight her mad dash for the hills seemed somewhat melodramatic, especially when Cameron proceeded to behave so normally, filling up the kettle to place it on the stove that was already lit.

She noticed a small box of groceries sitting on the dresser. 'When did you arrive?'

'Yesterday afternoon.' He reached up in cupboards for teacups and saucers. 'I flew Concorde early morning, got a plane from Heathrow to Inverness, and a hire car from there.'

Riona frowned. She understood he must have overtaken her on the way, but she had seen no sign of the hire car.

'I left the car with Dr Macnab,' he explained.

Riona nodded, then scowled as the penny dropped. If he'd arrived yesterday afternoon, the doctor had known he was here and waiting for her. She felt betrayed.

'Don't blame him.' Cameron read her mind as he turned to lean back against the sink. 'I told him what had happened and he, in turn, told me a few things. Then we both decided I should have a chance to sort out things between us without you taking flight again.'

Riona's mouth set into stubborn, sullen lines, as she repeated, 'I won't go back, Cameron.'

But if she expected an argument, he simply nodded. 'OK, that's understood. I guess I was crazy to think you could settle in Boston, even for a little while... I realised that well enough last summer.'

'Is that why you made up all those stories?' Riona asked in accusing tones.

'Stories?'

'About settling in Invergair and running the estate.'

'They weren't stories, Ree,' he claimed in reply. 'I saw my future with you, the two of us running the estate together.'

Riona shook her head, refusing to believe he'd meant that dream. 'You were never going to give up your life in Boston and your position in Harcourt Adams—just for Invergair.'

'No, not just for Invergair.' A look told her that once he would have given everything up for her.

Riona looked away. It was too late now, and she didn't want reminding of what she'd lost.

'Anyway,' he ran on, 'I have given it up...as of yesterday.'

Riona's eyes returned to his face. 'What do you mean?'

'What I said,' he answered unhelpfully, then kept her in suspense as he turned back to the stove to lift the kettle and pour hot water into the teapot. He carried it over on a tray with cups and saucers and sat down on the chair round the table from her.

He poured them both tea, before continuing, 'Of course, we'll have to come to some arrangement.'

'Arrangement?'

'I think it's only fair I have Rory on weekends,' he said with stunning composure.

Riona erupted immediately, 'But I'm *not* going back to Boston!'

'No? Well, neither am I,' he informed her, and, at her look of mystification, went on blandly, 'I thought I'd just said. I'm coming back to Invergair—to run the estate as planned.'

Riona's heart sank like a stone. 'So you and Melissa will be setting up home in Invergair Hall?'

'*Melissa*?' He looked surprised, then gave a derisive laugh. 'Can you really see Melissa living there? From memory, the plumbing alone would have her running back to Boston.'

'Then you'll be building a new house,' Riona concluded, and tried hard to seem indifferent, while inside she was devastated.

He shrugged. 'I don't know. It might be possible to bring Invergair Hall into the twentieth century without losing its character. What do you think?' He lifted a quizzical brow in her direction.

'I...' Riona didn't want to discuss the home he planned sharing with someone else. 'I don't think it's any of my business.'

'No, probably not,' he agreed, 'though that doesn't usually stop you expressing an opinion.'

Riona's mouth compressed into a thin line. 'I'm hardly in a position to do so. After all, it seems I'm back to being your tenant.'

'True,' he conceded. 'Which, of course, means I have some interest in your future intentions. For instance, do you plan to run the croft on your own or is there some man waiting in the wings?'

'Man? What man?' Riona snapped at this absurdity.

'I don't know.' His tone remained studiously neutral. 'There's Fergus Ross. Presumably he'll come home again and then——'

'Forget it!' Riona cut in sharply. 'Fergus and I are over for good. It's just you who keeps dragging his name up.'

'Only because you've never really told me about him,' he countered in response.

But if it was an invitation for Riona to reveal all, she turned it down. Talking about Fergus would simply cause more bitterness between them.

Cameron, however, wasn't about to let it go. 'As a matter of fact, Dr Macnab has tried to set me straight about your sailor friend. Or, at least, about the night I drove him up here. The doc says you let him sleep on your couch because it was too late for him to go home. He says you were never really serious about Fergus, just obligated.'

'And you believe him?' Somehow Riona doubted it.

'I don't know.' His eyes rested on her face, as if he might read the truth there. 'You tell me.'

But Riona refused to play his game, whatever it was. 'What's the point? It doesn't——'

'If you say it doesn't matter——' Cameron took the words out of her mouth '—just once more, Riona Macleod, I swear I'll do something crazy... crazier even than chasing you halfway across the world! So let's have it straight. What's Fergus Ross to you?' he demanded in a tone that warned her to push him no further.

'Nothing.' Riona threw the word back at him, then, tired of the whole business, relayed flatly, 'I went to school with Fergus, and only knew him slightly. The winter my grandfather was ill, he came home on leave.' She paused for breath, and her face reflected the misery of that time. 'My grandfather, he wanted to die at home, and I couldn't manage on my own. Fergus helped...'

'He was in love with you,' Cameron concluded with a hard edge.

Riona shook her head. 'He said he was, but it was just words.'

'And you?' Cameron watched conflicting emotions chase across her face.

'I thought I was,' she admitted almost fiercely, 'but it wasn't real. I slept with him, though, and that's what you want to know. I was grateful to him, and I was lonely, and I slept with him. Is that so terrible?' she demanded, even as the tears collected at the back of her eyes.

She waited for condemnation from Cameron. None came. Instead a hand reached out to gently touch her face. 'No, it's not so terrible,' he agreed quietly. 'I just wished you'd told me.'

'I tried.' A tear slipped down her face and was rubbed away by a long, tapered finger. 'I tried, but you thought I was a virgin, and I felt if you knew the truth you wouldn't want me any more.' She confessed the absurdity of it in a rush.

'Want you?' He shut his eyes for a moment in a gesture of despair. 'Ree, I wanted you from the first day we met and I've never stopped wanting you. You must know that,' he urged, as she turned doubting eyes on him.

'What do you think the other night was about? I meant to wait, but I needed you too much. I haven't been able to touch another woman since you.'

'But Melissa——' Riona began to protest, only to be rudely cut off.

'God, would you shut up about Melissa?' Cameron finally lost patience, and, pushing away from the table, crossed back to the sink. Only when he had put distance between them did he continue, 'Do you really imagine I give a damn about Melissa?'

'I know you do.' Riona wondered why he was pretending otherwise. He didn't have to. 'Melissa told me——'

'A sight too much,' he interrupted in exasperation, 'but who can blame her, when she has such a receptive audience? Melissa plays games with people. Don't you understand that?'

'I'm not stupid,' Riona snapped back. 'I know she likes manipulating people, and hurting them. But that doesn't change the fact she wants to marry you, and you can't deny it.'

'Well, if she does,' he admitted the possibility, 'it's through nothing I've done. As far as I'm concerned, she's my stepsister, period... Yes, all right, you saw us together on Friday night, but really you saw nothing. I took Melissa away from the party because she was drunk and she made a totally unappealing pass at me. Satisfied?'

'But if you married her——' Riona still couldn't accept she was his wiling choice '—you'd get control over Harcourt Adams.'

'So? Has it ever occurred to you that I might not want Harcourt Adams?' he said in exasperation. 'My father sold his soul and married Barbara for control of the business. Do you think I want to do the same?'

'I don't know.' Riona was unconvinced.

'God, what do I need to do to prove it?' he appealed in frustration, then, without giving her the chance to answer, suggested, 'I could always marry you, as planned. Then maybe you'll believe me.'

'That's not funny!' Riona stood up and started to collect the tea things, a swath of blonde hair hiding the hurt on her face.

He moved out of her way as she came towards the sink, and allowed her to deposit the dishes, before catching hold of her arm. 'It wasn't meant to be funny, Ree,' he sighed back. 'Don't you get it yet? Come here.'

Gently he tried to pull her round towards him, but Riona resisted, steeling herself against him. 'Don't start that again. It's not fair.'

'Why not?' He lifted a hand to caress the back of her neck, making her shiver. 'If it's the only way I can have you——'

'No.' She jerked back from him, and came up hard against the dresser. 'I don't want to. Not any more.'

'Don't you?' He moved in on her, an arm trapping her at each side, not touching, not needing to. 'You'll always want me, Ree. Just as I'll always want you. It's the way things are.'

With nowhere to run, Riona begged him, 'Stop doing this to me, Cameron.'

'Doing what?' He lifted a hand to touch her cheek, and she visibly trembled.

'Using me!' she cried out against her own weakness. 'You think because I'm a nobody it's OK for you to treat me how you like.'

'A nobody?' he repeated in disbelief.

'Not rich like your family,' she added, 'or socially acceptable or——'

He interrupted her with a short, harsh laugh. 'Oh, I get it. You mean poor little defenceless Riona with no one to protect her from the big bad American? Is that really how you see us?'

He laughed again, and, bristling with temper, Riona tried to break free from his hold. He pushed her back against the dresser.

'Well, don't kid yourself,' he told her, straight. 'You give as good as you get, Riona Macleod, and I've got the scars to prove it. Sure, I got it wrong about Fergus. I admit that. But it was hardly surprising. There was me, acting like a lovesick adolescent, spilling my guts out to you, planning our lives together, and all the time you're stringing me along, not once telling me what you really felt,' he finished angrily, his hands holding her arms painfully tight.

'B-but...' Riona stammered in protest '...*you* walked out on *me*.'

'Why do you think?' he demanded, but didn't wait for an answer. 'You don't imagine it was just finding about Fergus? He made me see, that's all. There he was, hitching in the dark, desperate to get home to *his* girl, so sure of you—just as I'd been. That's when I realised you'd never said it. A dozen times I'd told you I loved you, and not once had you ever said it back.'

Riona shook her head. She had said it. She must have. She'd showed it, anyway. Hadn't it been obvious?

Not to Cameron, it seemed, as he continued harshly, 'Well, I guess I'll have to live with the fact, because you're going to marry me whether you like it or not, Riona Macleod.'

'I...' Riona stared at him in hope. 'Are you saying... saying that you...?'

'I'm not saying anything,' he told her roughly.

But Riona needed the words. 'You're saying you *want* to marry me?'

'What else?' he growled in less than lover-like tones.

Riona's doubts returned. 'It's Rory, isn't it? You're marrying me for his sake.'

'God, you still don't get it yet, do you?' Cameron swore under his breath at her obtuseness. 'Then let me spell it out for you. I left here, hating you. I spent a year trying to shut you out of my mind. Yet I was on a plane to Britain within a day of hearing you'd had a baby.'

'You knew before you returned?' Riona hadn't realised that.

'Yeah, I knew,' he admitted roughly. 'What do you think brought me back? And no, it wasn't to play Daddy. I just thought—I've got her ... If it's mine, I've got her.'

'But *you* left *me* ...' Riona still didn't understand.

'Of course I left!' he almost shouted at her. 'If I hadn't, I would have killed you. Or, worse, I would have got down on my knees and begged you to choose me, not Ross. So I got out, while I still had some pride, some sanity. But then I heard about Rory and it gave me the chance to come back, to demand, not beg, believing your position made you helpless. I thought, I can have her without admitting I love her—to anybody, including myself. I can pretend I'm doing what's right, and forget it's the only thing I can do, when life without you is impossible. I——'

'Don't say any more.' Riona looked at him with wonder as she finally understood. He was handing her his pride—the pride that had demanded he leave her—and she wanted to weep for the waste of it, a year of their lives together lost.

'I think, Cameron,' she went on softly, 'it's my turn to say it. I loved you last summer, and when you left I thought I would die. I love you now. I'll always love you.'

His eyes ran over her beautiful face and saw her love, as true and simple and painful as his own.

'I do mean it,' she promised. 'I love you. I love you. I——'

The words were stolen from her, caught in her throat as he bent his head to touch his lips to hers. It was a special kiss, of love rather than passion, a kiss to seal the lifetime they finally realised they would spend together. When it threatened to turn into something else, he broke off and set her at arm's length. So often they had made love when they should have talked.

'You love me,' he repeated, and, at her nod of confirmation, laughed aloud. 'She puts me through hell, then tells me she loves me.'

'*I* put *you* through hell?' Riona protested at the nerve of it, and proved love hadn't made her completely soft as she recounted, 'So who jumped to conclusions, and went stomping off back to America? And who——?'

'Told me Rory wasn't mine,' he reminded her of one of her worst offences, although his wry tone suggested she'd been forgiven it, forgiven everything.

'Only because I thought you'd not want him,' Riona confessed in turn.

'Oh, I want him all right, but I want you more.' He reached out to cup her face. 'You see, Riona Macleod, you're in my blood and in my heart, and without you I know I'm nothing.'

He meant every word, as he confessed himself vulnerable, yet it was his strength Riona saw, and his strength she loved.

'Then be honest,' she pleaded. 'You have me, now and for always. The rest is up to you—Boston or Invergair?'

'You'd return?' he said in disbelief.

'Yes, I'd return. I realise I'm not the best executive wife material——' she smiled weakly at this understatement '—but I'd do my best to fit in.'

'You wouldn't fit in. Not in a million years,' he claimed, but a broad smile told her he loved her for the fact. 'And I don't want you to. I've wasted twelve years of my life with Harcourt Adams, doing a job that bores me rigid, mostly to please my father. And all the time my natural inheritance was here, on land that my mother's family worked four hundred years before Harcourt Adams was ever founded.'

'Are you sure?' Riona was scared to start believing again in the dream.

'Sure as I am of my love for you.' He kissed her brow with a tenderness that turned her heart over.

Riona struggled to hold on to reality. 'But what about your family?'

'You can be sure Barbara won't cry too many tears,' he commented drily, 'and Melissa will marry some other poor sucker and make his life a misery. My father...well, I've already talked it over with him. He gave me the choice. He'd hand over the running of Harcourt Adams to me now in the hope of ensuring my succession...or he'd give me his blessing and wish me well. I took the blessing.'

'He didn't mind?' Riona wondered at his father's generosity.

'I expect he did,' Cameron admitted, 'but he understood well enough. I guess he remembers what it was like to love a Scottish girl so much he could hardly bear to live without her.'

For the first time Cameron mentioned his father's grief at the loss of his mother, and Riona felt a terrible sadness for both, aware that a second marriage had never really filled the void.

'He'll miss you,' she said quietly.

'I'll miss him, too,' Cameron responded, 'but my life's here with you and Rory, and the sooner we get started on it, the better. So, why don't we go get our son and take him home to Invergair Hall?' he suggested, and held out a hand to her.

Riona hesitated a moment, realising what he was asking. If she went home with him now, the whole of Invergair would be talking of it tomorrow. But would that matter?

She slipped her hand in his as she decided, no, it didn't matter. Nothing mattered but that they wasted no more time apart.

They closed up the crofthouse and took the rough track over the hill to the village. They talked of the past and the future, and laughed together as they had before.

Then they stopped by the side of the Gair waterfall and he drew her down in the heather and she went, and they wrapped their arms round each other, and made love slowly, knowing now they would have a lifetime of being together like this.

They married three weeks later. Riona would have settled for a quiet Register Office wedding, but Cameron, who didn't care much for what people might say, insisted on a service in the village church. She wore a bridal suit of bright pink and Cameron wore a kilt that made him the most handsome Scot there. His father flew over to be best man, and the doctor gave her away. The church was packed with tenants and estate workers, happy to see the 'laird' marry one of their own. If the wedding was later than it should have been—for wasn't the father of Riona's baby now obvious?—then the gossip said that at least he was doing right by her finally.

Riona didn't care. She walked up the aisle with eyes only for Cameron and a heart singing with joy. He turned at the altar and the look on his face told her all she needed to know.

Their love wasn't dream, but reality. It wasn't gentle breezes, but a brisk wind. Not warm and safe and kind, but fierce and wild and...

All the sweeter for it.

HARLEQUIN®
PRESENTS Plus

Nathan Parnell needs a wife and mother for his young son. Sasha Redford and her daughter need a home. It's a match made in heaven, although no one's discussed the small matter of love.

Emily Musgrave and her nephew are on the run. But has she compounded her problems by accepting the help of Sandy McPherson, a total stranger?

Fall in love with Nathan and Sandy—Sasha and Emily do!

Watch for

In Need of a Wife by Emma Darcy
Harlequin Presents Plus #1679

and

Catch Me If You Can by Anne McAllister
Harlequin Presents Plus #1680

Harlequin Presents Plus
The best has just gotten better!

Available in September wherever Harlequin books are sold.